PPL
29.95

W9-ABR-014

c 1

SUMMER

Edith Wharton

G.K. Hall & Co. • **Chivers Press**
Thorndike, Maine USA **Bath, Avon, England**

PICKERING PUBLIC LIBRARY
CENTRAL BRANCH

This Large Print edition is published by G.K. Hall & Co., USA
and by Chivers Press, England.

U.S. Hardcover 0-7838-1831-9 (Perennial Bestseller Collection Edition)
U.K. Hardcover 0-7451-4997-9 (Chivers Large Print)
U.K. Softcover   0-7451-4998-7 (Camden Large Print)

This book was originally published in 1917.

All rights reserved.

The text of this Large Print edition is unabridged.
Other aspects of the book may vary from the original edition.

Set in 16 pt. Bookman Old Style by Minnie B. Raven.

Printed in the United States on permanent paper.

British Library Cataloguing in Publication Data available.

Library of Congress Cataloging in Publication Data

Wharton, Edith, 1862–1937.
    Summer / Edith Wharton.
        p.   cm.
    ISBN 0-7838-1831-9 (lg. print : hc)
    1. Man–woman relationships — Massachusetts — Berkshire Hills —
Fiction. 2. Guardian and ward — Massachusetts — Fiction. 3. Young
women — Massachusetts — Fiction. 4. Large type books. I. Title.
[PS3545.H16S86   1996]
    813'.52—dc20   96-19299

ROXBURY PUBLIC LIBRARY
CENTRAL BRANCH

SUMMER

I

A girl came out of lawyer Royall's house, at the end of the one street of North Dormer, and stood on the doorstep.

It was the beginning of a June afternoon. The spring-like transparent sky shed a rain of silver sunshine on the roofs of the village, and on the pastures and larchwoods surrounding it. A little wind moved among the round white clouds on the shoulders of the hills, driving their shadows across the fields and down the grassy road that takes the name of street when it passes through North Dormer. The place lies high and in the open, and lacks the lavish shade of the more protected New England villages. The clump of weeping-willows about the duck pond, and the Norway spruces in front of the Hatchard gate, cast almost the only roadside shadow between lawyer Royall's house and the point where, at the other end of the village, the road rises above the church and skirts the black hemlock wall enclosing the cemetery.

The little June wind, frisking down the street, shook the doleful fringes of the

Hatchard spruces, caught the straw hat of a young man just passing under them, and spun it clean across the road into the duck-pond.

As he ran to fish it out the girl on lawyer Royall's doorstep noticed that he was a stranger, that he wore city clothes, and that he was laughing with all his teeth, as the young and careless laugh at such mishaps.

Her heart contracted a little, and the shrinking that sometimes came over her when she saw people with holiday faces made her draw back into the house and pretend to look for the key that she knew she had already put into her pocket. A narrow greenish mirror with a gilt eagle over it hung on the passage wall, and she looked critically at her reflection, wished for the thousandth time that she had blue eyes like Annabel Balch, the girl who sometimes came from Springfield to spend a week with old Miss Hatchard, straightened the sun-burnt hat over her small swarthy face, and turned out again into the sunshine.

"How I hate everything!" she murmured.

The young man had passed through the Hatchard gate, and she had the street to herself. North Dormer is at all times an empty place, and at three o'clock on a June afternoon its few able-bodied men are off in the fields or woods, and the women indoors, engaged in languid household drudgery.

The girl walked along, swinging her key on a finger, and looking about her with the heightened attention produced by the presence of a stranger in a familiar place. What, she wondered, did North Dormer look like to people from other parts of the world? She herself had lived there since the age of five, and had long supposed it to be a place of some importance. But about a year before, Mr. Miles, the new Episcopal clergyman at Hepburn, who drove over every other Sunday — when the roads were not ploughed up by hauling — to hold a service in the North Dormer church, had proposed, in a fit of missionary zeal, to take the young people down to Nettleton to hear an illustrated lecture on the Holy Land; and the dozen girls and boys who represented the future of North Dormer had been piled into a farm-waggon, driven over the hills to Hepburn, put into a way-train and carried to Nettleton. In the course of that incredible day Charity Royall had, for the first and only time, experienced railway-travel, looked into shops with plate-glass fronts, tasted cocoanut pie, sat in a theatre, and listened to a gentleman saying unintelligible things before pictures that she would have enjoyed looking at if his explanations had not prevented her from understanding them. This initiation had shown her that North Dormer was a small place, and developed in her a thirst for information that her position as custodian of the village library had previously failed to excite. For a month or two she dipped feverishly and disconnectedly into the dusty volumes of the Hatchard Memorial Library; then the impression of Nettleton began to fade, and she found it easier to take North Dormer as the norm of the universe than to go on reading.

The sight of the stranger once more revived memories of Nettleton, and North Dormer shrank to its real size. As she looked up and down it, from lawyer Royall's faded red house at one end to the white church at the other, she pitilessly took its measure. There it lay, a weather-beaten sunburnt village of the hills, abandoned of men, left apart by railway, trolley, telegraph, and all the forces that link life to life in modern communities. It had no shops, no theatres, no lectures, no "business block"; only a church that was opened every other Sunday if the state of the roads permitted, and a library for which no new books had been bought for twenty years, and where the old ones mouldered undisturbed on the damp shelves. Yet Charity Royall had always been told that she ought to consider it a privilege that her lot had been cast in North Dormer. She knew that, compared to the place she had come from,

North Dormer represented all the blessings of the most refined civilization. Everyone in the village had told her so ever since she had been brought there as a child. Even old Miss Hatchard had said to her, on a terrible occasion in her life: "My child, you must never cease to remember that it was Mr. Royall who brought you down from the Mountain."

She had been "brought down from the Mountain"; from the scarred cliff that lifted its sullen wall above the lesser slopes of Eagle Range, making a perpetual background of gloom to the lonely valley. The Mountain was a good fifteen miles away, but it rose so abruptly from the lower hills that it seemed almost to cast its shadow over North Dormer. And it was like a great magnet drawing the clouds and scattering them in storm across the valley. If ever, in the purest summer sky, there trailed a thread of vapour over North Dormer, it drifted to the Mountain as a ship drifts to a whirlpool, and was caught among the rocks, torn up and multiplied, to sweep back over the village in rain and darkness.

Charity was not very clear about the Mountain; but she knew it was a bad place, and a shame to have come from, and that, whatever befell her in North Dormer, she ought, as Miss Hatchard had once reminded her, to remember that she had been brought down from there, and hold her tongue and be thankful. She looked up at the Mountain, thinking of these things, and tried as usual to be thankful. But the sight of the young man turning in at Miss Hatchard's gate had brought back the vision of the glittering streets of Nettleton, and she felt ashamed of her old sun-hat, and sick of North Dormer, and jealously aware of Annabel Balch of Springfield, opening her blue eyes somewhere far off on glories greater than the glories of Nettleton.

"How I hate everything!" she said again.

Half way down the street she stopped at a weak-hinged gate. Passing through it, she walked down a brick path to a queer little brick temple with white wooden columns supporting a pediment on which was inscribed in tarnished gold letters: "The Honorius Hatchard Memorial Library, 1832."

Honorius Hatchard had been old Miss Hatchard's great-uncle; though she would undoubtedly have reversed the phrase, and put forward, as her only claim to distinction, the fact that she was his great-niece. For Honorius Hatchard, in the early years of the nineteenth century, had enjoyed a modest celebrity. As the marble tablet in the interior of the library informed its infrequent visitors, he had possessed marked literary gifts, written a series of papers called "The

Recluse of Eagle Range," enjoyed the acquaintance of Washington Irving and Fitz-Greene Halleck, and been cut off in his flower by a fever contracted in Italy. Such had been the sole link between North Dormer and literature, a link piously commemorated by the erection of the monument where Charity Royall, every Tuesday and Thursday afternoon, sat at her desk under a freckled steel engraving of the deceased author, and wondered if he felt any deader in his grave than she did in his library.

Entering her prison-house with a listless step she took off her hat, hung it on a plaster bust of Minerva, opened the shutters, leaned out to see if there were any eggs in the swallow's nest above one of the windows, and finally, seating herself behind the desk, drew out a roll of cotton lace and a steel crochet hook. She was not an expert workwoman, and it had taken her many weeks to make the half-yard of narrow lace which she kept wound about the buckram back of a disintegrated copy of "The Lamplighter." But there was no other way of getting any lace to trim her summer blouse, and since Ally Hawes, the poorest girl in the village, had shown herself in church with enviable transparencies about the shoulders, Charity's hook had travelled faster. She unrolled the lace, dug the hook into a loop, and bent to the task with furrowed brows.

Suddenly the door opened, and before she had raised her eyes she knew that the young man she had seen going in at the Hatchard gate had entered the library.

Without taking any notice of her he began to move slowly about the long vault-like room, his hands behind his back, his short-sighted eyes peering up and down the rows of rusty bindings. At length he reached the desk and stood before her.

"Have you a card-catalogue?" he asked in a pleasant abrupt voice; and the oddness of the question caused her to drop her work.

"A *what?*"

"Why, you know —" He broke off, and she became conscious that he was looking at her for the first time, having apparently, on his entrance, included her in his general short-sighted survey as part of the furniture of the library.

The fact that, in discovering her, he lost the thread of his remark, did not escape her attention, and she looked down and smiled. He smiled also.

"No, I don't suppose you *do* know," he corrected himself. "In fact, it would be almost a pity —"

She thought she detected a slight condescension in his tone, and asked sharply: "Why?"

"Because it's so much pleasanter, in a small library like this, to poke about by

14

one's self — with the help of the librarian."

He added the last phrase so respectfully that she was mollified, and rejoined with a sigh: "I'm afraid I can't help you much."

"Why?" he questioned in his turn; and she replied that there weren't many books anyhow, and that she'd hardly read any of them. "The worms are getting at them," she added gloomily.

"Are they? That's a pity, for I see there are some good ones." He seemed to have lost interest in their conversation, and strolled away again, apparently forgetting her. His indifference nettled her, and she picked up her work, resolved not to offer him the least assistance. Apparently he did not need it, for he spent a long time with his back to her, lifting down, one after another, the tall cobwebby volumes from a distant shelf.

"Oh, I say!" he exclaimed; and looking up she saw that he had drawn out his handkerchief and was carefully wiping the edges of the book in his hand. The action struck her as an unwarranted criticism on her care of the books, and she said irritably: "It's not my fault if they're dirty."

He turned around and looked at her with reviving interest. "Ah — then you're not the librarian?"

"Of course I am; but I can't dust all these books. Besides, nobody ever looks at them, now Miss Hatchard's too lame to come round."

"No, I suppose not." He laid down the book he had been wiping, and stood considering her in silence. She wondered if Miss Hatchard had sent him around to pry into the way the library was looked after, and the suspicion increased her resentment. "I saw you going into her house just now, didn't I?" she asked, with the New England avoidance of the proper name. She was determined to find out why he was poking about among her books.

"Miss Hatchard's house? Yes — she's my cousin and I'm staying there," the young man answered; adding, as if to disarm a visible distrust: "My name is Harney — Lucius Harney. She may have spoken of me."

"No, she hasn't," said Charity, wishing she could have said: "Yes, she has."

"Oh, well —" said Miss Hatchard's cousin with a laugh; and after another pause, during which it occurred to Charity that her answer had not been encouraging, he remarked: "You don't seem strong on architecture."

Her bewilderment was complete: the more she wished to appear to understand him the more unintelligible his remarks became. He reminded her of the gentleman who had "explained" the pictures at Nettleton, and the weight of her ignorance settled down on her again like a pall.

"I mean, I can't see that you have any books on the old houses about here. I suppose, for that matter, this part of the country hasn't been much explored. They all go on doing Plymouth and Salem. So stupid. My cousin's house, now, is remarkable. This place must have had a past — it must have been more of a place once." He stopped short, with the blush of a shy man who overhears himself, and fears he has been voluble. "I'm an architect, you see, and I'm hunting up old houses in these parts."

She stared. "Old houses? Everything's old in North Dormer, isn't it? The folks are, anyhow."

He laughed, and wandered away again.

"Haven't you any kind of a history of the place? I think there was one written about 1840: a book or pamphlet about its first settlement," he presently said from the farther end of the room.

She pressed her crochet hook against her lip and pondered. There was such a work, she knew: "North Dormer and the Early Townships of Eagle County." She had a special grudge against it because it was a limp weakly book that was always either falling off the shelf or slipping back and disappearing if one squeezed it in between sustaining volumes. She remembered, the last time she

17

had picked it up, wondering how anyone could have taken the trouble to write a book about North Dormer and its neighbours: Dormer, Hamblin, Creston and Creston River. She knew them all, mere lost clusters of houses in the folds of the desolate ridges: Dormer, where North Dormer went for its apples; Creston River, where there used to be a papermill, and its grey walls stood decaying by the stream; and Hamblin, where the first snow always fell. Such were their titles to fame.

She got up and began to move about vaguely before the shelves. But she had no idea where she had last put the book, and something told her that it was going to play her its usual trick and remain invisible. It was not one of her lucky days.

"I guess it's somewhere," she said, to prove her zeal; but she spoke without conviction, and felt that her words conveyed none.

"Oh, well —" he said again. She knew he was going, and wished more than ever to find the book.

"It will be for next time," he added; and picking up the volume he had laid on the desk he handed it to her. "By the way, a little air and sun would do this good; it's rather valuable."

He gave her a nod and smile, and passed out.

II

The hours of the Hatchard Memorial librarian were from three to five; and Charity Royall's sense of duty usually kept her at her desk until nearly half-past four.

But she had never perceived that any practical advantage thereby accrued either to North Dormer or to herself; and she had no scruple in decreeing, when it suited her, that the library should close an hour earlier. A few minutes after Mr. Harney's departure she formed this decision, put away her lace, fastened the shutters, and turned the key in the door of the temple of knowledge.

The street upon which she emerged was still empty: and after glancing up and down it she began to walk toward her house. But instead of entering she passed on, turned into a field-path and mounted to a pasture on the hillside. She let down the bars of the gate, followed a trail along the crumbling wall of the pasture, and walked on till she reached a knoll where a clump of larches shook out their fresh tassels to the wind. There she lay down on the slope, tossed off her hat and hid her face in the grass.

She was blind and insensible to many things, and dimly knew it; but to all that was light and air, perfume and colour, every drop of blood in her responded. She loved the roughness of the dry mountain grass under her palms, the smell of the thyme into which she crushed her face, the fingering of the wind in her hair and through her cotton blouse, and the creak of the larches as they swayed to it.

She often climbed up the hill and lay there alone for the mere pleasure of feeling the wind and of rubbing her cheeks in the grass. Generally at such times she did not think of anything, but lay immersed in an inarticulate well-being. Today the sense of well-being was intensified by her joy at escaping from the library. She liked well enough to have a friend drop in and talk to her when she was on duty, but she hated to be bothered about books. How could she remember where they were, when they were so seldom asked for? Orma Fry occasionally took out a novel, and her brother Ben was fond of what he called "jography," and of books relating to trade and bookkeeping; but no one else asked for anything except, at intervals, "Uncle Tom's Cabin," or "Opening of a Chestnut Burr," or Longfellow. She had these under her hand, and could have found them in the dark; but unexpected demands came so rarely that they exasperated her like an injustice. . . .

She had liked the young man's looks, and his short-sighted eyes, and his odd way of speaking, that was abrupt yet soft, just as his hands were sunburnt and sinewy, yet with smooth nails like a woman's. His hair was sunburnt-looking too, or rather the colour of bracken after frost; his eyes grey, with the appealing look of the short-sighted, his smile shy yet confident, as if he knew lots of things she had never dreamed of, and yet wouldn't for the world have had her feel his superiority. But she did feel it, and liked the feeling; for it was new to her. Poor and ignorant as she was, and knew herself to be — humblest of the humble even in North Dormer, where to come from the Mountain was the worst disgrace — yet in her narrow world she had always ruled. It was partly, of course, owing to the fact that lawyer Royall was "the biggest man in North Dormer"; so much too big for it, in fact, that outsiders, who didn't know, always wondered how it held him. In spite of everything — and in spite even of Miss Hatchard — lawyer Royall ruled in North Dormer; and Charity ruled in lawyer Royall's house. She had never put it to herself in those terms; but she knew her power, knew what it was made of, and hated it. Confusedly, the young man in the library had made her feel

for the first time what might be the sweetness of dependence.

She sat up, brushed the bits of grass from
her hair, and looked down on the house
where she held sway. It stood just below
her, cheerless and untended, its faded red
front divided from the road by a "yard" with
a path bordered by gooseberry bushes, a
stone well overgrown with traveller's joy,
and a sickly Crimson Rambler tied to a
fan-shaped support, which Mr. Royall had
once brought up from Hepburn to please
her. Behind the house a bit of uneven
ground with clothes-lines strung across it
stretched up to a dry wall, and beyond the
wall a patch of corn and a few rows of
potatoes strayed vaguely into the adjoining
wilderness of rock and fern.

Charity could not recall her first sight of
the house. She had been told that she was
ill of a fever when she was brought down
from the Mountain; and she could only
remember waking one day in a cot at the
foot of Mrs. Royall's bed, and opening her
eyes on the cold neatness of the room that
was afterward to be hers.

Mrs. Royall died seven or eight years later;
and by that time Charity had taken the
measure of most things about her. She
knew that Mrs. Royall was sad and timid
and weak; she knew that lawyer Royall was
harsh and violent, and still weaker. She

knew that she had been christened Charity (in the white church at the other end of the village) to commemorate Mr. Royall's disinterestedness in "bringing her down," and to keep alive in her a becoming sense of her dependence; she knew that Mr. Royall was her guardian, but that he had not legally adopted her, though everybody spoke of her as Charity Royall; and she knew why he had come back to live at North Dormer, instead of practising at Nettleton, where he had begun his legal career.

After Mrs. Royall's death there was some talk of sending her to a boarding-school. Miss Hatchard suggested it, and had a long conference with Mr. Royall, who, in pursuance of her plan, departed one day for Starkfield to visit the institution she recommended. He came back the next night with a black face; worse, Charity observed, than she had ever seen him; and by that time she had had some experience.

When she asked him how soon she was to start he answered shortly, "You ain't going," and shut himself up in the room he called his office; and the next day the lady who kept the school at Starkfield wrote that "under the circumstances" she was afraid she could not make room just then for another pupil.

Charity was disappointed; but she understood. It wasn't the temptations of Starkfield that had been Mr. Royall's undoing; it was the thought of losing her. He was a dreadfully "lonesome" man; she had made that out because she was so "lonesome" herself. He and she, face to face in that sad house, had sounded the depths of isolation; and though she felt no particular affection for him, and not the slightest gratitude, she pitied him because she was conscious that he was superior to the people about him, and that she was the only being between him and solitude. Therefore, when Miss Hatchard sent for her a day or two later, to talk of a school at Nettleton, and to say that this time a friend of hers would "make the necessary arrangements," Charity cut her short with the announcement that she had decided not to leave North Dormer.

Miss Hatchard reasoned with her kindly, but to no purpose; she simply repeated: "I guess Mr. Royall's too lonesome."

Miss Hatchard blinked perplexedly behind her eyeglasses. Her long frail face was full of puzzled wrinkles, and she leant forward, resting her hands on the arms of her mahogany armchair, with the evident desire to say something that ought to be said.

"The feeling does you credit, my dear."

She looked about the pale walls of her sitting-room, seeking counsel of ancestral daguerreotypes and didactic samplers; but

they seemed to make utterance more difficult.

"The fact is, it's not only — not only
because of the advantages. There are other
reasons. You're too young to understand —"

"Oh, no, I ain't," said Charity harshly; and
Miss Hatchard blushed to the roots of her
blonde cap. But she must have felt a vague
relief at having her explanation cut short,
for she concluded, again invoking the daguerreotypes: "Of course I shall always do
what I can for you; and in case . . . in case
. . . you know you can always come to
me. . . ."

Lawyer Royall was waiting for Charity on
the porch when she returned from this visit.
He had shaved, and brushed his black coat,
and looked a magnificent monument of a
man; at such moments she really admired
him.

"Well," he said, "is it settled?"

"Yes, it's settled. I ain't going."

"Not to the Nettleton school?"

"Not anywhere."

He cleared his throat and asked sternly:
"Why?"

"I'd rather not," she said, swinging past
him on her way to her room. It was the
following week that he brought her up the
Crimson Rambler and its fan from Hepburn.
He had never given her anything before.

The next outstanding incident of her life had happened two years later, when she was seventeen. Lawyer Royall, who hated to go to Nettleton, had been called there in connection with a case. He still exercised his profession, though litigation languished in North Dormer and its outlying hamlets; and for once he had had an opportunity that he could not afford to refuse. He spent three days in Nettleton, won his case, and came back in high good-humour. It was a rare mood with him, and manifested itself on this occasion by his talking impressively at the supper-table of the "rousing welcome" his old friends had given him. He wound up confidentially: "I was a damn fool ever to leave Nettleton. It was Mrs. Royall that made me do it."

Charity immediately perceived that something bitter had happened to him, and that he was trying to talk down the recollection. She went up to bed early, leaving him seated in moody thought, his elbows propped on the worn oilcloth of the supper-table. On the way up she had extracted from his overcoat pocket the key of the cupboard where the bottle of whiskey was kept.

She was awakened by a rattling at her door and jumped out of bed. She heard Mr. Royall's voice, low and peremptory, and opened the door, fearing an accident. No other thought had occurred to her; but when she saw him in the doorway, a ray from the autumn moon falling on his discomposed face, she understood.

For a moment they looked at each other in silence; then, as he put his foot across the threshold, she stretched out her arm and stopped him.

"You go right back from here," she said, in a shrill voice that startled her; "you ain't going to have that key tonight."

"Charity, let me in. I don't want the key. I'm a lonesome man," he began, in the deep voice that sometimes moved her.

Her heart gave a startled plunge, but she continued to hold him back contemptuously. "Well, I guess you made a mistake, then. This ain't your wife's room any longer."

She was not frightened, she simply felt a deep disgust; and perhaps he divined it or read it in her face, for after staring at her a moment he drew back and turned slowly away from the door. With her ear to her keyhole she heard him feel his way down the dark stairs, and toward the kitchen; and she listened for the crash of the cupboard panel, but instead she heard him, after an interval, unlock the door of the house, and his heavy steps came to her through the silence as he walked down the path. She crept to the window and saw his bent figure striding up the road in the moonlight. Then a belated sense of fear came to her with the consciousness of victory, and she slipped into bed, cold to the bone.

A day or two later poor Eudora Skeff, who for twenty years had been the custodian of the Hatchard library, died suddenly of pneumonia; and the day after the funeral Charity went to see Miss Hatchard, and asked to be appointed librarian. The request seemed to surprise Miss Hatchard: she evidently questioned the new candidate's qualifications.

"Why, I don't know, my dear. Aren't you rather too young?" she hesitated.

"I want to earn some money," Charity merely answered.

"Doesn't Mr. Royall give you all you require? No one is rich in North Dormer."

"I want to earn money enough to get away."

"To get away?" Miss Hatchard's puzzled wrinkles deepened, and there was a distressful pause. "You want to leave Mr. Royall?"

"Yes: or I want another woman in the house with me," said Charity resolutely.

Miss Hatchard clasped her nervous hands about the arms of her chair. Her eyes invoked the faded countenances on the wall, and after a faint cough of indecision she brought out: "The . . . the housework's too hard for you, I suppose?"

Charity's heart grew cold. She understood that Miss Hatchard had no help to give her and that she would have to fight her way out of her difficulty alone. A deeper sense of isolation overcame her; she felt incalculably old. "She's got to be talked to like a baby," she thought, with a feeling of compassion for Miss Hatchard's long immaturity. "Yes, that's it," she said aloud. "The housework's too hard for me: I've been coughing a good deal this fall."

She noted the immediate effect of this suggestion. Miss Hatchard paled at the memory of poor Eudora's taking-off, and promised to do what she could. But of course there were people she must consult: the clergyman, the selectmen of North Dormer, and a distant Hatchard relative at Springfield. "If you'd only gone to school!" she sighed. She followed Charity to the door, and there, in the security of the threshold, said with a glance of evasive appeal: "I know Mr. Royall is . . . trying at times; but his wife bore with him; and you must always remember, Charity, that it was Mr. Royall who brought you down from the Mountain."

Charity went home and opened the door of Mr. Royall's "office." He was sitting there by the stove reading Daniel Webster's speeches. They had met at meals during the five days that had elapsed since he had come to her door, and she had walked at his side at Eudora's funeral; but they had not spoken a word to each other.

He glanced up in surprise as she entered, and she noticed that he was unshaved, and that he looked unusually old; but as she had always thought of him as an old man the change in his appearance did not move her. She told him she had been to see Miss Hatchard, and with what object. She saw that he was astonished; but he made no comment.

"I told her the housework was too hard for me, and I wanted to earn the money to pay for a hired girl. But I ain't going to pay for her: you've got to. I want to have some money of my own."

Mr. Royall's bushy black eyebrows were drawn together in a frown, and he sat drumming with ink-stained nails on the edge of his desk.

"What do you want to earn money for?" he asked.

"So's to get away when I want to."

"Why do you want to get away?"

Her contempt flashed out. "Do you suppose anybody'd stay at North Dormer if they could help it? You wouldn't, folks say!"

With lowered head he asked: "Where'd you go to?"

"Anywhere where I can earn my living. I'll try here first, and if I can't do it here I'll go somewhere else. I'll go up the Mountain if I have to." She paused on this threat, and saw that it had taken effect. "I want you should get Miss Hatchard and the selectmen to take me at the library: and I want a woman here in the house with me," she repeated.

Mr. Royall had grown exceedingly pale. When she ended he stood up ponderously, leaning against the desk; and for a second or two they looked at each other.

"See here," he said at length as though utterance were difficult, "there's something I've been wanting to say to you; I'd ought to have said it before. I want you to marry me."

The girl still stared at him without moving. "I want you to marry me," he repeated, clearing his throat. "The minister'll be up here next Sunday and we can fix it up then. Or I'll drive you down to Hepburn to the Justice, and get it done there. I'll do whatever you say." His eyes fell under the merciless stare she continued to fix on him, and he shifted his weight uneasily from one foot to the other. As he stood there before her, unwieldy, shabby, disordered, the purple veins distorting the hands he pressed against the desk, and his long orator's jaw trembling with the effort of his avowal, he seemed like a hideous parody of the fatherly old man she had always known.

"Marry you? Me?" she burst out with a scornful laugh. "Was that what you came to ask me the other night? What's come over you, I wonder? How long is it since you've looked at yourself in the glass?" She straightened herself, insolently conscious of her youth and strength. "I suppose you think it would be cheaper to marry me than to keep a hired girl. Everybody knows you're the closest man in Eagle County; but I guess you're not going to get your mending done for you that way twice."

Mr. Royall did not move while she spoke. His face was ash-coloured and his black eyebrows quivered as though the blaze of her scorn had blinded him. When she ceased he held up his hand.

"That'll do — that'll about do," he said. He turned to the door and took his hat from the hat-peg. On the threshold he paused. "People ain't been fair to me — from the first they ain't been fair to me," he said. Then he went out.

A few days later North Dormer learned with surprise that Charity had been appointed librarian of the Hatchard Memorial at a salary of eight dollars a month, and that old Verena Marsh, from the Creston Almshouse, was coming to live at lawyer Royall's and do the cooking.

III

It was not in the room known at the red house as Mr. Royall's "office" that he received his infrequent clients. Professional dignity and masculine independence made it necessary that he should have a real office, under a different roof; and his standing as the only lawyer of North Dormer required that the roof should be the same as that which sheltered the Town Hall and the post-office.

It was his habit to walk to this office twice a day, morning and afternoon. It was on the ground floor of the building, with a separate entrance, and a weathered name-plate on the door. Before going in he stepped in to the post-office for his mail — usually an empty ceremony — said a word or two to the town-clerk, who sat across the passage in idle state, and then went over to the store on the opposite corner, where Carrick Fry, the storekeeper, always kept a chair for him, and where he was sure to find one or two selectmen leaning on the long counter, in an atmosphere of rope, leather, tar and coffee-beans. Mr. Royall, though monosyllabic at home, was not averse, in certain moods, to imparting his views to his fellow-townsmen; perhaps, also, he was unwilling that his rare clients should surprise him sitting, clerkless and unoccupied, in his dusty office. At any rate, his hours there were not much longer or more regular than Charity's at the library; the rest of the time he spent either at the store or in driving about the country on business connected with the insurance companies that he represented, or in sitting at home reading Bancroft's History of the United States and the speeches of Daniel Webster.

Since the day when Charity had told him that she wished to succeed to Eudora Skeff's post their relations had undefinably but definitely changed. Lawyer Royall had kept his word. He had obtained the place for her at the cost of considerable manœuvering, as she guessed from the number of rival candidates, and from the acerbity with which two of them, Orma Fry and the eldest Targatt girl, treated her for nearly a year afterward. And he had engaged Verena Marsh to come up from Creston and do the cooking. Verena was a poor old widow, doddering and shiftless: Charity suspected that she came for her keep. Mr. Royall was too close a man to give a dollar a day to a smart girl when he could get a deaf pauper for nothing. But at any rate, Verena was there, in the attic just over Charity, and the fact that she was deaf did not greatly trouble the young girl.

Charity knew that what had happened on that hateful night would not happen again. She understood that, profoundly as she had despised Mr. Royall ever since, he despised himself still more profoundly. If she had asked for a woman in the house it was far less for her own defense than for his humiliation. She needed no one to defend her: his humbled pride was her surest protection. He had never spoken a word of excuse or extenuation; the incident was as if it had never been. Yet its consequences were latent in every word that he and she exchanged, in every glance they instinctively turned from each other. Nothing now would ever shake her rule in the red house.

On the night of her meeting with Miss Hatchard's cousin Charity lay in bed, her bare arms clasped under her rough head, and continued to think of him. She supposed that he meant to spend some time in North Dormer. He had said he was looking up the old houses in the neighbourhood; and though she was not very clear as to his purpose, or as to why anyone should look for old houses, when they lay in wait for one on every roadside, she understood that he needed the help of books,

35

and resolved to hunt up the next day the volume she had failed to find, and any others that seemed related to the subject.

Never had her ignorance of life and literature so weighed on her as in reliving the short scene of her discomfiture. "It's no use trying to be anything in this place," she muttered to her pillow; and she shrivelled at the vision of vague metropolises, shining super-Nettletons, where girls in better clothes than Belle Balch's talked fluently of architecture to young men with hands like Lucius Harney's. Then she remembered his sudden pause when he had come close to the desk and had his first look at her. The sight had made him forget what he was going to say; she recalled the change in his face, and jumping up she ran over the bare boards to her washstand, found the matches, lit a candle, and lifted it to the square of looking-glass on the whitewashed wall. Her small face, usually so darkly pale, glowed like a rose in the faint orb of light, and under her rumpled hair her eyes seemed deeper and larger than by day. Perhaps after all it was a mistake to wish they were blue. A clumsy band and button fastened her unbleached night-gown about the throat. She undid it, freed her thin shoulders, and saw herself a bride in low-necked satin, walking down an aisle with Lucius Harney. He would kiss her as they left the church. . . . She put down the candle and covered her face with her hands as if to imprison the kiss. At that moment she heard Mr. Royall's step as he came up the stairs to bed, and a fierce revulsion of feeling swept over her. Until then she had merely despised him; now deep hatred of him filled her heart. He became to her a horrible old man. . . .

The next day, when Mr. Royall came back to dinner, they faced each other in silence as usual. Verena's presence at the table was an excuse for their not talking, though her deafness would have permitted the freest interchange of confidences. But when the meal was over, and Mr. Royall rose from the table, he looked back at Charity, who had stayed to help the old woman clear away the dishes.

"I want to speak to you a minute," he said; and she followed him across the passage, wondering.

He seated himself in his black horse-hair armchair, and she leaned against the window, indifferently. She was impatient to be gone to the library, to hunt for the book on North Dormer.

"See here," he said, "why ain't you at the library the days you're supposed to be there?"

The question, breaking in on her mood of

blissful abstraction, deprived her of speech, and she stared at him for a moment without answering.

"Who says I ain't?"

"There's been some complaints made, it appears. Miss Hatchard sent for me this morning —"

Charity's smouldering resentment broke into a blaze. "I know! Orma Fry, and that toad of a Targatt girl — and Ben Fry, like as not. He's going round with her. The low-down sneaks — I always knew they'd try to have me out! As if anybody ever came to the library, anyhow!"

"Somebody did yesterday, and you weren't there."

"Yesterday?" she laughed at her happy recollection. "At what time wasn't I there yesterday, I'd like to know?"

"Round about four o'clock."

Charity was silent. She had been so steeped in the dreamy remembrance of young Harney's visit that she had forgotten having deserted her post as soon as he had left the library.

"Who came at four o'clock?"

"Miss Hatchard did."

"Miss Hatchard? Why, she ain't ever been near the place since she's been lame. She couldn't get up the steps if she tried."

"She can be helped up, I guess. She was yesterday, anyhow, by the young fellow that's staying with her. He found you there, I understand, earlier in the afternoon; and he went back and told Miss Hatchard the books were in bad shape and needed attending to. She got excited, and had herself wheeled straight round; and when she got there the place was locked. So she sent for me, and told me about that, and about the other complaints. She claims you've neglected things, and that she's going to get a trained librarian."

Charity had not moved while he spoke. She stood with her head thrown back against the window-frame, her arms hanging against her sides, and her hands so tightly clenched that she felt, without knowing what hurt her, the sharp edge of her nails against her palms.

Of all Mr. Royall had said she had retained only the phrase: "He told Miss Hatchard the books were in bad shape." What did she care for the other charges against her? Malice or truth, she despised them as she despised her detractors. But that the stranger to whom she had felt herself so mysteriously drawn should have betrayed her! That at the very moment when she had fled up the hillside to think of him more deliciously he should have been hastening home to denounce her shortcomings! She remembered how, in the darkness of her room, she had covered her face to press his imagined kiss closer; and her heart raged against him for the liberty he had not taken.

"Well, I'll go," she said suddenly. "I'll go right off."

"Go where?" She heard the startled note in Mr. Royall's voice.

"Why, out of their old library: straight out, and never set foot in it again. They needn't think I'm going to wait round and let them say they've discharged me!"

"Charity — Charity Royall, you listen —" he began, getting heavily out of his chair; but she waved him aside, and walked out of the room.

Upstairs she took the library key from the place where she always hid it under her pincushion — who said she wasn't careful? — put on her hat, and swept down again and out into the street. If Mr. Royall heard her go he made no motion to detain her: his sudden rages probably made him understand the uselessness of reasoning with hers.

She reached the brick temple, unlocked the door and entered into the glacial twilight. "I'm glad I'll never have to sit in this old vault again when other folks are out in the sun!" she said aloud as the familiar chill took her. She looked with abhorrence at the long dingy rows of books, the sheep-nosed Minerva on her black pedestal, and the mild-faced young man in a high stock whose effigy pined above her desk. She meant to take out of the drawer her roll of lace and the library register, and go straight to Miss Hatchard to announce her resignation. But suddenly a great desolation overcame her, and she sat down and laid her face against the desk. Her heart was ravaged by life's cruelest discovery: the first creature who had come toward her out of the wilderness had brought her anguish instead of joy. She did not cry; tears came hard to her, and the storms of her heart spent themselves inwardly. But as she sat there in her dumb woe she felt her life to be too desolate, too ugly and intolerable.

"What have I ever done to it, that it should hurt me so?" she groaned, and pressed her fists against her lids, which were beginning to swell with weeping.

"I won't — I won't go there looking like a horror!" she muttered, springing up and pushing back her hair as if it stifled her. She opened the drawer, dragged out the register, and turned toward the door. As she did so it opened, and the young man from Miss Hatchard's came in whistling.

IV

He stopped and lifted his hat with a shy smile. "I beg your pardon," he said. "I thought there was no one here."

Charity stood before him, barring his way. "You can't come in. The library ain't open to the public Wednesdays."

"I know it's not; but my cousin gave me her key."

"Miss Hatchard's got no right to give her key to other folks, any more'n I have. I'm the librarian and I know the by-laws. This is my library."

The young man looked profoundly surprised.

"Why, I know it is; I'm so sorry if you mind my coming."

"I suppose you came to see what more you could say to set her against me? But you needn't trouble: it's my library today, but it won't be this time tomorrow. I'm on the way now to take her back the key and the register."

Young Harney's face grew grave, but without betraying the consciousness of guilt she had looked for.

"I don't understand," he said. "There must be some mistake. Why should I say things against you to Miss Hatchard — or to anyone?"

The apparent evasiveness of the reply caused Charity's indignation to overflow. "I don't know why you should. I could understand Orma Fry's doing it, because she's always wanted to get me out of here ever since the first day. I can't see why, when she's got her own home, and her father to work for her; nor Ida Targatt, neither, when she got a legacy from her step-brother on'y last year. But anyway we all live in the same place, and when it's a place like North Dormer it's enough to make people hate each other just to have to walk down the same street every day. But you don't live here, and you don't know anything about any of us, so what did you have to meddle for? Do you suppose the other girls'd have kept the books any better'n I did? Why, Orma Fry don't hardly know a book from a flat-iron! And what if I don't always sit round here doing nothing till it strikes five up at the church? Who cares if the library's open or shut? Do you suppose anybody ever comes here for books? What they'd like to come for is to meet the fellows they're going with — if I'd let 'em. But I wouldn't let Bill Sollas from over the hill hang round here waiting for the youngest Targatt girl, because I know him . . . that's all . . . even if I don't know about books all I ought to. . . ."

She stopped with a choking in her throat. Tremors of rage were running through her, and she steadied herself against the edge of the desk lest he should see her weakness.

What he saw seemed to affect him deeply, for he grew red under his sunburn, and stammered out: "But, Miss Royall, I assure you . . . I assure you . . ."

His distress inflamed her anger, and she regained her voice to fling back: "If I was you I'd have the nerve to stick to what I said!"

The taunt seemed to restore his presence of mind. "I hope I should if I knew; but I don't. Apparently something disagreeable has happened, for which you think I'm to blame. But I don't know what it is, because I've been up on Eagle Ridge ever since the early morning."

"I don't know where you've been this morning, but I know you were here in this library yesterday; and it was you that went home and told your cousin the books were in bad shape, and brought her round to see how I'd neglected them."

Young Harney looked sincerely concerned. "Was that what you were told? I don't wonder you're angry. The books *are* in bad shape, and as some are interesting it's a pity. I told Miss Hatchard they were suffering from dampness and lack of air; and I brought her here to show her how easily the place could be ventilated. I also told her you ought to have some one to help you do the dusting and airing. If you were given a wrong version of what I said I'm sorry; but I'm so fond of old books that I'd rather see them made into a bonfire than left to moulder away like these."

Charity felt her sobs rising and tried to stifle them in words. "I don't care what you say you told her. All I know is she thinks it's all my fault, and I'm going to lose my job, and I wanted it more'n anyone in the village, because I haven't got anybody belonging to me, the way other folks have. All I wanted was to put aside money enough to get away from here sometime. D'you suppose if it hadn't been for that I'd have kept on sitting day after day in this old vault?"

Of this appeal her hearer took up only the last question. "It *is* an old vault; but need it be? That's the point. And it's my putting the question to my cousin that seems to have been the cause of the trouble." His glance explored the melancholy penumbra of the long narrow room, resting on the blotched walls, the discoloured rows of books, and the stern rosewood desk surmounted by the portrait of the young Honorius. "Of course it's a bad job to do anything with a building jammed against a hill like this ridiculous mausoleum: you couldn't get a good draught through it without blowing a hole in the mountain. But it can be ventilated after a fashion, and the sun can be let in: I'll show you how if you like. . . ." The architect's passion for improvement had already made him lose sight of her grievance, and he lifted his stick instructively toward the cornice. But her silence seemed to tell him that she took no interest in the ventilation of the library, and turning back to her abruptly he held out both hands. "Look here — you don't mean what you said? You don't really think I'd do anything to hurt you?"

A new note in his voice disarmed her: no one had ever spoken to her in that tone.

"Oh, what *did* you do it for then?" she wailed. He had her hands in his, and she was feeling the smooth touch that she had imagined the day before on the hillside.

He pressed her hands lightly and let them go. "Why, to make things pleasanter for you here; and better for the books. I'm sorry if my cousin twisted around what I said. She's excitable, and she lives on trifles: I ought to have remembered that. Don't punish me by letting her think you take her seriously."

It was wonderful to hear him speak of Miss Hatchard as if she were a querulous baby: in spite of his shyness he had the air of power that the experience of cities probably gave. It was the fact of having lived in Nettleton that made lawyer Royall, in spite of his infirmities, the strongest man in North Dormer; and Charity was sure that this young man had lived in bigger places than Nettleton.

She felt that if she kept up her denunciatory tone he would secretly class her with Miss Hatchard; and the thought made her suddenly simple.

"It don't matter to Miss Hatchard how I take her. Mr. Royall says she's going to get a trained librarian; and I'd sooner resign than have the village say she sent me away."

"Naturally you would. But I'm sure she doesn't mean to send you away. At any rate, won't you give me the chance to find out first and let you know? It will be time enough to resign if I'm mistaken."

Her pride flamed into her cheeks at the suggestion of his intervening. "I don't want anybody should coax her to keep me if I don't suit."

He coloured too. "I give you my word I won't do that. Only wait till tomorrow, will you?" He looked straight into her eyes with his shy grey glance. "You can trust me, you know — you really can."

All the old frozen woes seemed to melt in her, and she murmured awkwardly, looking away from him: "Oh, I'll wait."

V

There had never been such a June in Eagle County. Usually it was a month of moods, with abrupt alternations of belated frost and mid-summer heat; this year, day followed day in a sequence of temperate beauty. Every morning a breeze blew steadily from the hills. Toward noon it built up great canopies of white cloud that threw a cool shadow over fields and woods; then before sunset the clouds dissolved again, and the western light rained its unobstructed brightness on the valley.

On such an afternoon Charity Royall lay on a ridge above a sunlit hollow, her face pressed to the earth and the warm currents of the grass running through her. Directly in her line of vision a blackberry branch laid its frail white flowers and blue-green leaves against the sky. Just beyond, a tuft of sweet-fern uncurled between the beaded shoots of the grass, and a small yellow butterfly vibrated over them like a fleck of sunshine. This was all she saw; but she felt, above her and about her, the strong growth of the beeches clothing the ridge,

48

the rounding of pale green cones on count-less spruce-branches, the push of myriads of sweet-fern fronds in the cracks of the stony slope below the wood, and the crowd-ing shoots of meadowsweet and yellow flags in the pasture beyond. All this bubbling of sap and slipping of sheaths and bursting of calyxes was carried to her on mingled currents of fragrance. Every leaf and bud and blade seemed to contribute its exhala-tion to the pervading sweetness in which the pungency of pine-sap prevailed over the spice of thyme and the subtle perfume of fern, and all were merged in a moist earth-smell that was like the breath of some huge sun-warmed animal.

Charity had lain there a long time, passive and sun-warmed as the slope on which she lay, when there came between her eyes and the dancing butterfly the sight of a man's foot in a large worn boot covered with red mud.

"Oh, don't!" she exclaimed, raising herself on her elbow and stretching out a warning hand.

"Don't what?" a hoarse voice asked above her head.

"Don't stamp on those bramble flowers, you dolt!" she retorted, springing to her knees. The foot paused and then descended clumsily on the frail branch, and raising her eyes she saw above her the bewildered

face of a slouching man with a thin sunburnt beard, and white arms showing
through his ragged shirt.

"Don't you ever *see* anything, Liff Hyatt?"
she assailed him, as he stood before her
with the look of a man who has stirred up
a wasp's nest.

He grinned. "I seen you! That's what I
come down for."

"Down from where?" she questioned,
stooping to gather up the petals his foot
had scattered.

He jerked his thumb toward the heights.
"Been cutting down trees for Dan Targatt."

Charity sank back on her heels and
looked at him musingly. She was not in the
least afraid of poor Liff Hyatt, though he
"came from the Mountain," and some of
the girls ran when they saw him. Among
the more reasonable he passed for a harmless creature, a sort of link between the
Mountain and civilized folk, who occasionally came down and did a little wood-cutting for a farmer when hands were short.
Besides, she knew the Mountain people
would never hurt her: Liff himself had told
her so once when she was a little girl, and
had met him one day at the edge of lawyer
Royall's pasture. "They won't any of 'em
touch you up there, f'ever you was to come
up. . . . But I don't s'pose you will," he had
added philosophically, looking at her new

50

shoes, and at the red ribbon that Mrs. Royall had tied in her hair.

Charity had, in truth, never felt any desire to visit her birthplace. She did not care to have it known that she was of the Mountain, and was shy of being seen in talk with Liff Hyatt. But today she was not sorry to have him appear. A great many things had happened to her since the day when young Lucius Harney had entered the doors of the Hatchard Memorial, but none, perhaps, so unforeseen as the fact of her suddenly finding it a convenience to be on good terms with Liff Hyatt. She continued to look up curiously at his freckled weather-beaten face, with feverish hollows below the cheekbones and the pale yellow eyes of a harmless animal. "I wonder if he's related to me?" she thought, with a shiver of disdain.

"Is there any folks living in the brown house by the swamp, up under Porcupine?" she presently asked in an indifferent tone.

Liff Hyatt, for a while, considered her with surprise; then he scratched his head and shifted his weight from one tattered sole to the other.

"There's always the same folks in the brown house," he said with his vague grin.

"They're from up your way, ain't they?"

"Their name's the same as mine," he rejoined uncertainly.

Charity still held him with resolute eyes.

"See here, I want to go there some day and take a gentleman with me that's boarding with us. He's up in these parts drawing pictures."

She did not offer to explain this statement. It was too far beyond Liff Hyatt's limitations for the attempt to be worth making. "He wants to see the brown house, and go all over it," she pursued.

Liff was still running his fingers perplexedly through his shock of straw-coloured hair. "Is it a fellow from the city?" he asked.

"Yes. He draws pictures of things. He's down there now drawing the Bonner house." She pointed to a chimney just visible over the dip of the pasture below the wood.

"The Bonner house?" Liff echoed incredulously.

"Yes. You won't understand — and it don't matter. All I say is: he's going to the Hyatts' in a day or two."

Liff looked more and more perplexed. "Bash is ugly sometimes in the afternoons."

"I know. But I guess he won't trouble me." She threw her head back, her eyes full on Hyatt's. "I'm coming too: you tell him."

"They won't none of them trouble you, the Hyatts won't. What d'you want a take a stranger with you, though?"

"I've told you, haven't I? You've got to tell Bash Hyatt."

52

He looked away at the blue mountains on the horizon; then his gaze dropped to the chimney-top below the pasture.

"He's down there now?"

"Yes."

He shifted his weight again, crossed his arms, and continued to survey the distant landscape. "Well, so long," he said at last, inconclusively; and turning away he shambled up the hillside. From the ledge above her, he paused to call down: "I wouldn't go there a Sunday"; then he clambered on till the trees closed in on him. Presently, from high overhead, Charity heard the ring of his axe.

She lay on the warm ridge, thinking of many things that the woodsman's appearance had stirred up in her. She knew nothing of her early life, and had never felt any curiosity about it: only a sullen reluctance to explore the corner of her memory where certain blurred images lingered. But all that had happened to her within the last few weeks had stirred her to the sleeping depths. She had become absorbingly interesting to herself, and everything that had to do with her past was illuminated by this sudden curiosity.

She hated more than ever the fact of coming from the Mountain; but it was no longer indifferent to her. Everything that in any way affected her was alive and vivid: even the hateful things had grown interesting because they were a part of herself.

"I wonder if Liff Hyatt knows who my mother was?" she mused; and it filled her with a tremor of surprise to think that some woman who was once young and slight, with quick motions of the blood like hers, had carried her on her breast, and watched her sleeping. She had always thought of her mother as so long dead as to be no more than a nameless pinch of earth; but now it occurred to her that the once-young woman might be alive, and wrinkled and elf-locked like the woman she had sometimes seen in the door of the brown house that Lucius Harney wanted to draw.

The thought brought him back to the central point in her mind, and she strayed away from the conjectures roused by Liff Hyatt's presence. Speculations concerning the past could not hold her long when the present was so rich, the future so rosy, and when Lucius Harney, a stone's throw away, was bending over his sketch-book, frowning, calculating, measuring, and then throwing his head back with the sudden smile that had shed its brightness over everything.

She scrambled to her feet, but as she did so she saw him coming up the pasture and dropped down on the grass to wait. When he was drawing and measuring one of "his houses," as she called them, she often strayed away by herself into the woods or up the hillside. It was partly from shyness that she did so: from a sense of inadequacy that came to her most painfully when her companion, absorbed in his job, forgot her ignorance and her inability to follow his least allusion, and plunged into a mono- logue on art and life. To avoid the awkward- ness of listening with a blank face, and also to escape the surprised stare of the inhabi- tants of the houses before which he would abruptly pull up their horse and open his sketch-book, she slipped away to some spot from which, without being seen, she could watch him at work, or at least look down on the house he was drawing. She had not been displeased, at first, to have it known to North Dormer and the neighbourhood that she was driving Miss Hatchard's cousin about the country in the buggy he had hired of lawyer Royall. She had always kept to herself, contemptuously aloof from village love-making, without exactly know- ing whether her fierce pride was due to the sense of her tainted origin, or whether she was reserving herself for a more brilliant fate. Sometimes she envied the other girls their sentimental preoccupations, their long hours of inarticulate philandering with one of the few youths who still lingered in the village; but when she pictured herself curling her hair or putting a new ribbon on her hat for Ben Fry or one of the Sollas boys the fever dropped and she relapsed into indifference.

Now she knew the meaning of her disdains and reluctances. She had learned what she was worth when Lucius Harney, looking at her for the first time, had lost the thread of his speech, and leaned reddening on the edge of her desk. But another kind of shyness had been born in her: a terror of exposing to vulgar perils the sacred treasure of her happiness. She was not sorry to have the neighbours suspect her of "going with" a young man from the city, but she did not want it known to all the countryside how many hours of the long June days she spent with him. What she most feared was that the inevitable comments should reach Mr. Royall. Charity was instinctively aware that few things concerning her escaped the eyes of the silent man under whose roof she lived; and in spite of the latitude which North Dormer accorded to courting couples she had always felt that, on the day when she showed too open a preference, Mr. Royall might, as she phrased it, make her "pay for it." How, she did not know; and her fear was the greater because it was undefinable. If she had been accepting the attentions of one of the village youths she would have been less apprehensive: Mr. Royall could not prevent her marrying when she chose to. But everybody knew that "going with a city fellow" was a different and less straightforward affair: almost every village could show a victim of the perilous venture. And her dread of Mr. Royall's intervention gave a sharpened joy to the hours she spent with young Harney, and made her, at the same time, shy of being too generally seen with him.

As he approached she rose to her knees, stretching her arms above her head with the indolent gesture that was her way of expressing a profound well-being.

"I'm going to take you to that house up under Porcupine," she announced.

"What house? Oh, yes; that ramshackle place near the swamp, with the gipsy-looking people hanging about. It's curious that a house with traces of real architecture should have been built in such a place. But the people were a sulky-looking lot — do you suppose they'll let us in?"

"They'll do whatever I tell them," she said with assurance.

He threw himself down beside her. "Will they?" he rejoined with a smile. "Well, I should like to see what's left inside the house. And I should like to have a talk with the people. Who was it who was telling me the other day that they had come down from the Mountain?"

Charity shot a sideward look at him. It was the first time he had spoken of the Mountain except as a feature of the landscape. What else did he know about it, and about her relation to it? Her heart began to beat with the fierce impulse of resistance which she instinctively opposed to every imagined slight.

"The Mountain? I ain't afraid of the Mountain!"

Her tone of defiance seemed to escape him. He lay breast-down on the grass, breaking off sprigs of thyme and pressing them against his lips. Far off, above the folds of the nearer hills, the Mountain thrust itself up menacingly against a yellow sunset.

"I must go up there some day: I want to see it," he continued.

Her heart-beats slackened and she turned again to examine his profile. It was innocent of all unfriendly intention.

"What'd you want to go up the Mountain for?"

"Why, it must be rather a curious place. There's a queer colony up there, you know: sort of outlaws, a little independent kingdom. Of course you've heard them spoken of; but I'm told they have nothing to do with the people in the valleys — rather look down on them, in fact. I suppose they're rough customers; but they must have a good deal of character."

She did not quite know what he meant by having a good deal of character; but his tone was expressive of admiration, and deepened her dawning curiosity. It struck her now as strange that she knew so little about the Mountain. She had never asked, and no one had ever offered to enlighten her. North Dormer took the Mountain for granted, and implied its disparagement by an intonation rather than by explicit criticism.

"It's queer, you know," he continued, "that, just over there, on top of that hill, there should be a handful of people who don't give a damn for anybody."

The words thrilled her. They seemed the clue to her own revolts and defiances, and she longed to have him tell her more.

"I don't know much about them. Have they always been there?"

"Nobody seems to know exactly how long. Down at Creston they told me that the first colonists are supposed to have been men who worked on the railway that was built forty or fifty years ago between Springfield and Nettleton. Some of them took to drink, or got into trouble with the police, and went off — disappeared into the woods. A year or two later there was a report that they were living up on the Mountain. Then I suppose others joined them — and children were born. Now they say there are over a hundred people up there. They seem to be quite outside the jurisdiction of the valleys. No school, no church — and no sheriff ever goes up to see what they're about. But don't people ever talk of them at North Dormer?"

"I don't know. They say they're bad."

He laughed. "Do they? We'll go and see, shall we?"

She flushed at the suggestion, and turned her face to his. "You never heard, I suppose — I come from there. They brought me down when I was little."

"You?" He raised himself on his elbow, looking at her with sudden interest. "You're from the Mountain? How curious! I suppose that's why you're so different. . . ."

Her happy blood bathed her to the forehead. He was praising her — and praising her because she came from the Mountain!

"Am I . . . different?" she triumphed, with affected wonder.

"Oh, awfully!" He picked up her hand and laid a kiss on the sunburnt knuckles.

"Come," he said, "let's be off." He stood up and shook the grass from his loose grey clothes. "What a good day! Where are you going to take me tomorrow?"

VI

That evening after supper Charity sat alone in the kitchen and listened to Mr. Royall and young Harney talking on the porch.

She had remained indoors after the table had been cleared and old Verena had hobbled up to bed. The kitchen window was open, and Charity seated herself near it, her idle hands on her knee. The evening was cool and still. Beyond the black hills an amber west passed into pale green, and then to a deep blue in which a great star hung. The soft hoot of a little owl came through the dusk, and between its calls the men's voices rose and fell.

Mr. Royall's was full of a sonorous satisfaction. It was a long time since he had had anyone of Lucius Harney's quality to talk to: Charity divined that the young man symbolized all his ruined and unforgotten past. When Miss Hatchard had been called to Springfield by the illness of a widowed sister, and young Harney, by that time seriously embarked on his task of drawing and measuring all the old houses between

Nettleton and the New Hampshire border, had suggested the possibility of boarding at the red house in his cousin's absence, Charity had trembled lest Mr. Royall should refuse. There had been no question of lodging the young man: there was no room for him. But it appeared that he could still live at Miss Hatchard's if Mr. Royall would let him take his meals at the red house; and after a day's deliberation Mr. Royall consented.

Charity suspected him of being glad of the chance to make a little money. He had the reputation of being an avaricious man; but she was beginning to think he was probably poorer than people knew. His practice had become little more than vague legend, revived only at lengthening intervals by a summons to Hepburn or Nettleton; and he appeared to depend for his living mainly on the scant produce of his farm, and on the commissions received from the few insurance agencies that he represented in the neighbourhood. At any rate, he had been prompt in accepting Harney's offer to hire the buggy at a dollar and a half a day; and his satisfaction with the bargain had manifested itself, unexpectedly enough, at the end of the first week, by his tossing a ten-dollar bill into Charity's lap as she sat one day re-trimming her old hat.

"Here — go get yourself a Sunday bonnet

that'll make all the other girls mad," he said, looking at her with a sheepish twinkle in his deep-set eyes; and she immediately guessed that the unwonted present — the only gift of money she had ever received from him — represented Harney's first payment.

But the young man's coming had brought Mr. Royall other than pecuniary benefit. It gave him, for the first time in years, a man's companionship. Charity had only a dim understanding of her guardian's needs; but she knew he felt himself above the people among whom he lived, and she saw that Lucius Harney thought him so. She was surprised to find how well he seemed to talk now that he had a listener who understood him; and she was equally struck by young Harney's friendly deference.

Their conversation was mostly about politics, and beyond her range; but tonight it had a peculiar interest for her, for they had begun to speak of the Mountain. She drew back a little, lest they should see she was in hearing.

"The Mountain? The Mountain?" she heard Mr. Royall say. "Why the Mountain's a blot — that's what it is, sir, a blot. That scum up there ought to have been run in long ago — and would have, if the people down here hadn't been clean scared of them. The Mountain belongs to this township, and it's North Dormer's fault if there's a gang of thieves and outlaws living over there, in sight of us, defying the laws of their country. Why, there ain't a sheriff or a tax-collector or a coroner'd durst go up there. When they hear of trouble on the Mountain the selectmen look the other way, and pass an appropriation to beautify the town pump. The only man that ever goes up is the minister, and he goes because they send down and get him whenever there's any of them dies. They think a lot of Christian burial on the Mountain — but I never heard of their having the minister up to marry them. And they never trouble the Justice of the Peace either. They just herd together like the heathen."

He went on, explaining in somewhat technical language how the little colony of squatters had contrived to keep the law at bay, and Charity, with burning eagerness, awaited young Harney's comment; but the young man seemed more concerned to hear Mr. Royall's views than to express his own.

"I suppose you've never been up there yourself?" he presently asked.

"Yes, I have," said Mr. Royall with a contemptuous laugh. "The wiseacres down here told me I'd be done for before I got back; but nobody lifted a finger to hurt me. And I'd just had one of their gang sent up for seven years too."

"You went up after that?"

"Yes, sir: right after it. The fellow came down to Nettleton and ran amuck, the way they sometimes do. After they've done a wood-cutting job they come down and blow the money in; and this man ended up with manslaughter. I got him convicted, though they were scared of the Mountain even at Nettleton; and then a queer thing happened. The fellow sent for me to go and see him in gaol. I went, and this is what he says: 'The fool that defended me is a chicken-livered son of a — and all the rest of it,' he says. 'I've got a job to be done for me up on the Mountain, and you're the only man I seen in court that looks as if he'd do it.' He told me he had a child up there — or thought he had — a little girl; and he wanted her brought down and reared like a Christian. I was sorry for the fellow, so I went up and got the child." He paused, and Charity listened with a throbbing heart. "That's the only time I ever went up the Mountain," he concluded.

There was a moment's silence; then Harney spoke. "And the child — had she no mother?"

"Oh, yes: there was a mother. But she was glad enough to have her go. She'd have given her to anybody. They ain't half human up there. I guess the mother's dead by now, with the life she was leading. Anyhow, I've

65

never heard of her from that day to this."

"My God, how ghastly," Harney murmured; and Charity, choking with humiliation, sprang to her feet and ran upstairs. She knew at last: knew that she was the child of a drunken convict and of a mother who wasn't "half human," and was glad to have her go; and she had heard this history of her origin related to the one being in whose eyes she longed to appear superior to the people about her! She had noticed that Mr. Royall had not named her, had even avoided any allusion that might identify her with the child he had brought down from the Mountain; and she knew it was out of regard for her that he had kept silent. But of what use was his discretion, since only that afternoon, misled by Harney's interest in the outlaw colony, she had boasted to him of coming from the Mountain? Now every word that had been spoken showed her how such an origin must widen the distance between them.

During his ten days' sojourn at North Dormer Lucius Harney had not spoken a word of love to her. He had intervened in her behalf with his cousin, and had convinced Miss Hatchard of her merits as a librarian; but that was a simple act of justice, since it was by his own fault that those merits had been questioned. He had asked her to drive him about the country when he hired lawyer Royall's buggy to go on his sketching expeditions; but that too was natural enough, since he was unfamiliar with the region. Lastly, when his cousin was called to Springfield, he had begged Mr. Royall to receive him as a boarder; but where else in North Dormer could he have boarded? Not with Carrick Fry, whose wife was paralysed, and whose large family crowded his table to over-flowing; not with the Targatts, who lived a mile up the road, nor with poor old Mrs. Hawes, who, since her eldest daughter had deserted her, barely had the strength to cook her own meals while Ally picked up her living as a seamstress. Mr. Royall's was the only house where the young man could have been offered a decent hospitality. There had been nothing, therefore, in the outward course of events to raise in Charity's breast the hopes with which it trembled. But beneath the visible incidents resulting from Lucius Harney's arrival there ran an undercurrent as mysterious and potent as the influence that makes the forest break into leaf before the ice is off the pools.

The business on which Harney had come was authentic; Charity had seen the letter from a New York publisher commissioning him to make a study of the eighteenth-century houses in the less familiar districts of New England. But incomprehensible as the whole affair was to her, and hard as she found it to understand why he paused enchanted before certain neglected and paintless houses, while others, refurbished and "improved" by the local builder, did not arrest a glance, she could not but suspect that Eagle County was less rich in architecture than he averred, and that the duration of his stay (which he had fixed at a month) was not unconnected with the look in his eyes when he had first paused before her in the library. Everything that had followed seemed to have grown out of that look: his way of speaking to her, his quickness in catching her meaning, his evident eagerness to prolong their excursions and to seize on every chance of being with her.

The signs of his liking were manifest enough; but it was hard to guess how much they meant, because his manner was so different from anything North Dormer had ever shown her. He was at once simpler and more deferential than any one she had known; and sometimes it was just when he was simplest that she most felt the distance between them. Education and opportunity had divided them by a width that no effort of hers could bridge, and even when his youth and his admiration brought him nearest, some chance word, some unconscious allusion, seemed to thrust her back across the gulf.

Never had it yawned so wide as when she fled up to her room carrying with her the echo of Mr. Royall's tale. Her first confused thought was the prayer that she might never see young Harney again. It was too bitter to picture him as the detached impartial listener to such a story. "I wish he'd go away: I wish he'd go tomorrow, and never come back!" she moaned to her pillow; and far into the night she lay there, in the disordered dress she had forgotten to take off, her whole soul a tossing misery on which her hopes and dreams spun about like drowning straws.

Of all this tumult only a vague heart-soreness was left when she opened her eyes the next morning. Her first thought was of the weather, for Harney had asked her to take him to the brown house under Porcupine, and then around by Hamblin; and as the trip was a long one they were to start at nine. The sun rose without a cloud, and earlier than usual she was in the kitchen, making cheese sandwiches, decanting buttermilk into a bottle, wrapping up slices of apple pie, and accusing Verena of having given away a basket she needed, which had always hung on a hook in the passage. When she came out into the porch, in her pink calico, which had run a little in the washing, but was still bright enough to set off her dark tints, she had such a triumphant sense of being a part of the sunlight and the morning that the last trace of her misery vanished. What did it matter where she came from, or whose child she was, when love was dancing in her veins, and down the road she saw young Harney coming toward her?

Mr. Royall was on the porch too. He had said nothing at breakfast, but when she came out in her pink dress, the basket in her hand, he looked at her with surprise. "Where you going to?" he asked.

"Why — Mr. Harney's starting earlier than usual today," she answered.

"Mr. Harney, Mr. Harney? Ain't Mr. Harney learned how to drive a horse yet?"

She made no answer, and he sat tilted back in his chair, drumming on the rail of the porch. It was the first time he had ever spoken of the young man in that tone, and Charity felt a faint chill of apprehension. After a moment he stood up and walked away toward the bit of ground behind the house, where the hired man was hoeing.

The air was cool and clear, with the autumnal sparkle that a north wind brings to the hills in early summer, and the night had been so still that the dew hung on everything, not as a lingering moisture, but in separate beads that glittered like diamonds on the ferns and grasses. It was a long drive to the foot of Porcupine: first across the valley, with blue hills bounding the open slopes; then down into the beach-woods, following the course of the Creston, a brown brook leaping over velvet ledges; then out again onto the farm-lands about Creston Lake, and gradually up the ridges of the Eagle Range. At last they reached the yoke of the hills, and before them opened another valley, green and wild, and beyond it more blue heights eddying away to the sky like the waves of a receding tide.

Harney tied the horse to a tree-stump, and they unpacked their basket under an aged walnut with a riven trunk out of which bumblebees darted. The sun had grown hot, and behind them was the noonday murmur of the forest. Summer insects danced on the air, and a flock of white butterflies fanned the mobile tips of the crimson fireweed. In the valley below not a house was visible; it seemed as if Charity Royall and young Harney were the only living beings in the great hollow of earth and sky.

Charity's spirits flagged and disquieting thoughts stole back on her. Young Harney had grown silent, and as he lay beside her, his arms under his head, his eyes on the network of leaves above him, she wondered if he were musing on what Mr. Royall had told him, and if it had really debased her in his thoughts. She wished he had not asked her to take him that day to the brown house; she did not want him to see the people she came from while the story of her birth was fresh in his mind. More than once she had been on the point of suggesting that they should follow the ridge and drive straight to Hamblin, where there was a little deserted house he wanted to see; but shyness and pride held her back. "He'd better know what kind of folks I belong to," she said to herself, with a somewhat forced defiance; for in reality it was shame that kept her silent.

Suddenly she lifted her hand and pointed to the sky. "There's a storm coming up."

He followed her glance and smiled. "Is it that scrap of cloud among the pines that frightens you?"

"It's over the Mountain; and a cloud over the Mountain always means trouble."

"Oh, I don't believe half the bad things you all say of the Mountain! But anyhow, we'll get down to the brown house before the rain comes."

He was not far wrong, for only a few isolated drops had fallen when they turned into the road under the shaggy flank of Porcupine, and came upon the brown house. It stood alone beside a swamp bordered with alder thickets and tall bulrushes. Not another dwelling was in sight, and it was hard to guess what motive could have actuated the early settler who had made his home in so unfriendly a spot.

Charity had picked up enough of her companion's erudition to understand what had attracted him to the house. She noticed the fan-shaped tracery of the broken light above the door, the flutings of the paintless pilasters at the corners, and the round window set in the gable; and she knew that, for reasons that still escaped her, these were things to be admired and recorded. Still, they had seen other houses far more "typical" (the word was Harney's); and as he threw the reins on the horse's neck he said with a slight shiver of repugnance: "We won't stay long."

Against the restless alders turning their white lining to the storm the house looked singularly desolate. The paint was almost gone from the clapboards, the window-panes were broken and patched with rags, and the garden was a poisonous tangle of nettles, burdocks and tall swamp-weeds over which big blue-bottles hummed.

At the sound of wheels a child with a tow-head and pale eyes like Liff Hyatt's peered over the fence and then slipped away behind an out-house. Harney jumped down and helped Charity out; and as he did so the rain broke on them. It came slantwise, on a furious gale, laying shrubs

73

and young trees flat, tearing off their leaves like an autumn storm, turning the road into a river, and making hissing pools of every hollow. Thunder rolled incessantly through the roar of the rain, and a strange glitter of light ran along the ground under the increasing blackness.

"Lucky we're here after all," Harney laughed. He fastened the horse under a half-roofless shed, and wrapping Charity in his coat ran with her to the house. The boy had not reappeared, and as there was no response to their knocks Harney turned the door-handle and they went in.

There were three people in the kitchen to which the door admitted them. An old woman with a handkerchief over her head was sitting by the window. She held a sickly-looking kitten on her knees, and whenever it jumped down and tried to limp away she stooped and lifted it back without any change of her aged, unnoticing face. Another woman, the unkempt creature that Charity had once noticed in driving by, stood leaning against the window-frame and stared at them; and near the stove an unshaved man in a tattered shirt sat on a barrel asleep.

The place was bare and miserable and the air heavy with the smell of dirt and stale tobacco. Charity's heart sank. Old derided tales of the Mountain people came back to

her, and the woman's stare was so discon-
certing, and the face of the sleeping man
so sodden and bestial, that her disgust was
tinged with a vague dread. She was not
afraid for herself; she knew the Hyatts
would not be likely to trouble her; but she
was not sure how they would treat a "city
fellow."

Lucius Harney would certainly have
laughed at her fears. He glanced about the
room, uttered a general "How are you?" to
which no one responded, and then asked
the younger woman if they might take shelter till the storm was over.

She turned her eyes away from him and
looked at Charity.

"You're the girl from Royall's, ain't you?"

The colour rose in Charity's face. "I'm
Charity Royall," she said, as if asserting her
right to the name in the very place where
it might have been most open to question.

The woman did not seem to notice. "You
kin stay," she merely said; then she turned
away and stooped over a dish in which she
was stirring something.

Harney and Charity sat down on a bench
made of a board resting on two starch
boxes. They faced a door hanging on a
broken hinge, and through the crack they
saw the eyes of the tow-headed boy and of
a pale little girl with a scar across her
cheek. Charity smiled, and signed to the

children to come in; but as soon as they saw they were discovered they slipped away on bare feet. It occurred to her that they were afraid of rousing the sleeping man; and probably the woman shared their fear, for she moved about as noiselessly and avoided going near the stove.

The rain continued to beat against the house, and in one or two places it sent a stream through the patched panes and ran into pools on the floor. Every now and then the kitten mewed and struggled down, and the old woman stooped and caught it, holding it tight in her bony hands; and once or twice the man on the barrel half woke, changed his position and dozed again, his head falling forward on his hairy breast. As the minutes passed, and the rain still streamed against the windows, a loathing of the place and the people came over Charity. The sight of the weak-minded old woman, of the cowed children, and the ragged man sleeping off his liquor, made the setting of her own life seem a vision of peace and plenty. She thought of the kitchen at Mr. Royall's, with its scrubbed floor and dresser full of china, and the peculiar smell of yeast and coffee and soft-soap that she had always hated, but that now seemed the very symbol of household order. She saw Mr. Royall's room, with the high-backed horsehair chair, the faded rag carpet, the row of books on a shelf, the engraving of "The Surrender of Burgoyne" over the stove, and the mat with a brown and white spaniel on a moss-green border. And then her mind travelled to Miss Hatchard's house, where all was freshness, purity and fragrance, and compared to which the red house had always seemed so poor and plain.

"This is where I belong — this is where I belong," she kept repeating to herself; but the words had no meaning for her. Every instinct and habit made her a stranger among these poor swamp-people living like vermin in their lair. With all her soul she wished she had not yielded to Harney's curiosity, and brought him there.

The rain had drenched her, and she began to shiver under the thin folds of her dress. The younger woman must have noticed it, for she went out of the room and came back with a broken teacup which she offered to Charity. It was half full of whiskey, and Charity shook her head; but Harney took the cup and put his lips to it. When he had set it down Charity saw him feel in his pocket and draw out a dollar; he hesitated a moment, and then put it back, and she guessed that he did not wish her to see him offering money to people she had spoken of as being her kin.

The sleeping man stirred, lifted his head

and opened his eyes. They rested vacantly for a moment on Charity and Harney, and then closed again, and his head drooped; but a look of anxiety came into the woman's face. She glanced out of the window and then came up to Harney. "I guess you better go along now," she said. The young man understood and got to his feet. "Thank you," he said, holding out his hand. She seemed not to notice the gesture, and turned away as they opened the door.

The rain was still coming down, but they hardly noticed it: the pure air was like balm in their faces. The clouds were rising and breaking, and between their edges the light streamed down from remote blue hollows. Harney untied the horse, and they drove off through the diminishing rain, which was already beaded with sunlight.

For a while Charity was silent, and her companion did not speak. She looked timidly at his profile: it was graver than usual, as though he too were oppressed by what they had seen. Then she broke out abruptly: "Those people back there are the kind of folks I come from. They may be my relations, for all I know." She did not want him to think that she regretted having told him her story.

"Poor creatures," he rejoined. "I wonder why they came down to that fever-hole."

She laughed ironically. "To better themselves! It's worse up on the Mountain. Bash Hyatt married the daughter of the farmer that used to own the brown house. That was him by the stove, I suppose."

Harney seemed to find nothing to say and she went on: "I saw you take out a dollar to give to that poor woman. Why did you put it back?"

He reddened, and leaned forward to flick a swamp-fly from the horse's neck. "I wasn't sure —"

"Was it because you knew they were my folks, and thought I'd be ashamed to see you give them money?"

He turned to her with eyes full of reproach. "Oh, Charity —" It was the first time he had ever called her by her name. Her misery welled over.

"I ain't — I ain't ashamed. They're my people, and I ain't ashamed of them," she sobbed.

"My dear . . ." he murmured, putting his arm about her; and she leaned against him and wept out her pain.

It was too late to go around to Hamblin, and all the stars were out in a clear sky when they reached the North Dormer valley and drove up to the red house.

VII

Since her reinstatement in Miss Hatchard's favour Charity had not dared to curtail by a moment her hours of attendance at the library. She even made a point of arriving before the time, and showed a laudable indignation when the youngest Targatt girl, who had been engaged to help in the cleaning and rearranging of the books, came trailing in late and neglected her task to peer through the window at the Sollas boy. Nevertheless, "library days" seemed more than ever irksome to Charity after her vivid hours of liberty; and she would have found it hard to set a good example to her subordinate if Lucius Harney had not been commissioned, before Miss Hatchard's departure, to examine with the local carpenter the best means of ventilating the "Memorial."

He was careful to prosecute this inquiry on the days when the library was open to the public; and Charity was therefore sure of spending part of the afternoon in his company. The Targatt girl's presence, and the risk of being interrupted by some passer-by suddenly smitten with a thirst for letters, restricted their intercourse to the exchange of commonplaces; but there was a fascination to Charity in the contrast between these public civilities and their secret intimacy.

The day after their drive to the brown house was "library day" and she sat at her desk working at the revised catalogue, while the Targatt girl, one eye on the window, chanted out the titles of a pile of books. Charity's thoughts were far away, in the dismal house by the swamp, and under the twilight sky during the long drive home, when Lucius Harney had consoled her with endearing words. That day, for the first time since he had been boarding with them, he had failed to appear as usual at the midday meal. No message had come to explain his absence, and Mr. Royall, who was more than usually taciturn, had betrayed no surprise, and made no comment. In itself this indifference was not particularly significant, for Mr. Royall, in common with most of his fellow-citizens, had a way of accepting events passively, as if he had long since come to the conclusion that no one who lived in North Dormer could hope to modify them. But to Charity, in the reaction from her mood of passionate exaltation, there was something disquieting in his silence. It was almost as if Lucius Harney had never had a part in their lives: Mr. Royall's imperturbable indifference seemed to relegate him to the domain of unreality.

As she sat at work, she tried to shake off her disappointment at Harney's non-appearing. Some trifling incident had probably kept him from joining them at midday; but she was sure he must be eager to see her again, and that he would not want to wait till they met at supper, between Mr. Royall and Verena. She was wondering what his first words would be, and trying to devise a way of getting rid of the Targatt girl before he came, when she heard steps outside, and he walked up the path with Mr. Miles.

The clergyman from Hepburn seldom came to North Dormer except when he drove over to officiate at the old white church which, by an unusual chance, happened to belong to the Episcopal communion. He was a brisk affable man, eager to make the most of the fact that a little nucleus of "church-people" had survived in the sectarian wilderness, and resolved to undermine the influence of the ginger-bread-coloured Baptist chapel at the other end of the village; but he was kept busy by parochial work at Hepburn, where there were papermills and saloons, and it was not often that he could spare time for North Dormer.

Charity, who went to the white church (like all the best people in North Dormer), admired Mr. Miles, and had even, during the memorable trip to Nettleton, imagined herself married to a man who had such a straight nose and such a beautiful way of speaking, and who lived in a brown-stone rectory covered with Virginia creeper. It had been a shock to discover that the privilege was already enjoyed by a lady with crimped hair and a large baby; but the arrival of Lucius Harney had long since banished Mr. Miles from Charity's dreams, and as he walked up the path at Harney's side she saw him as he really was: a fat middle-aged man with a baldness showing under his clerical hat, and spectacles on his Grecian nose. She wondered what had called him to North Dormer on a weekday, and felt a little hurt that Harney should have brought him to the library.

It presently appeared that his presence there was due to Miss Hatchard. He had been spending a few days at Springfield, to fill a friend's pulpit, and had been consulted by Miss Hatchard as to young Harney's plan for ventilating the "Memorial." To lay hands on the Hatchard ark was a grave matter, and Miss Hatchard, always full of scruples about her scruples (it was Harney's phrase), wished to have Mr. Miles's opinion before deciding.

"I couldn't," Mr. Miles explained, "quite make out from your cousin what changes you wanted to make, and as the other trustees did not understand either I thought I had better drive over and take a look — though I'm sure," he added, turning his friendly spectacles on the young man, "that no one could be more competent — but of course this spot has its peculiar sanctity!"

"I hope a little fresh air won't desecrate it," Harney laughingly rejoined; and they walked to the other end of the library while he set forth his idea to the Rector.

Mr. Miles had greeted the two girls with his usual friendliness, but Charity saw that he was occupied with other things, and she presently became aware, by the scraps of conversation drifting over to her, that he was still under the charm of his visit to Springfield, which appeared to have been full of agreeable incidents.

"Ah, the Coopersons . . . yes, you know them, of course," she heard. "That's a fine old house! And Ned Cooperson has collected some really remarkable impressionist pictures . . ." The names he cited were unknown to Charity. "Yes; yes; the Schaefer quartette played at Lyric Hall on Saturday evening; and on Monday I had the privilege of hearing them again at the Towers. Beautifully done . . . Bach and Beethoven . . . a

84

lawn-party first . . . I saw Miss Balch several times, by the way . . . looking extremely handsome. . . ."

Charity dropped her pencil and forgot to listen to the Targatt girl's sing-song. Why had Mr. Miles suddenly brought up Annabel Balch's name?

"Oh, really?" she heard Harney rejoin; and, raising his stick, he pursued: "You see, my plan is to move these shelves away, and open a round window in this wall, on the axis of the one under the pediment."

"I suppose she'll be coming up here later to stay with Miss Hatchard?" Mr. Miles went on, following on his train of thought; then, spinning about and tilting his head back: "Yes, yes, I see — I understand: that will give a draught without materially altering the look of things. I can see no objection."

The discussion went on for some minutes, and gradually the two men moved back toward the desk. Mr. Miles stopped again and looked thoughtfully at Charity. "Aren't you a little pale, my dear? Not overworking? Mr. Harney tells me you and Mamie are giving the library a thorough overhauling." He was always careful to remember his parishioners' Christian names, and at the right moment he bent his benignant spectacles on the Targatt girl.

Then he turned to Charity. "Don't take

things hard, my dear; don't take things hard. Come down and see Mrs. Miles and me some day at Hepburn," he said, pressing her hand and waving a farewell to Mamie Targatt. He went out of the library, and Harney followed him.

Charity thought she detected a look of constraint in Harney's eyes. She fancied he did not want to be alone with her; and with a sudden pang she wondered if he repented the tender things he had said to her the night before. His words had been more fraternal than loverlike; but she had lost their exact sense in the caressing warmth of his voice. He had made her feel that the fact of her being a waif from the Mountain was only another reason for holding her close and soothing her with consolatory murmurs; and when the drive was over, and she got out of the buggy, tired, cold, and aching with emotion, she stepped as if the ground were a sunlit wave and she the spray on its crest.

Why, then, had his manner suddenly changed, and why did he leave the library with Mr. Miles? Her restless imagination fastened on the name of Annabel Balch: from the moment it had been mentioned she fancied that Harney's expression had altered. Annabel Balch at a garden-party at Springfield, looking "extremely handsome" . . . perhaps Mr. Miles had seen her there at the very moment when Charity and Harney were sitting in the Hyatts' hovel, between a drunkard and a half-witted old woman! Charity did not know exactly what a garden-party was, but her glimpse of the flower-edged lawns of Nettleton helped her to visualize the scene, and envious recollections of the "old things" which Miss Balch avowedly "wore out" when she came to North Dormer made it only too easy to picture her in her splendour. Charity understood what associations the name must have called up, and felt the uselessness of struggling against the unseen influences in Harney's life.

When she came down from her room for supper he was not there; and while she waited on the porch she recalled the tone in which Mr. Royall had commented the day before on their early start. Mr. Royall sat at her side, his chair tilted back, his broad black boots with side-elastics resting against the lower bar of the railings. His rumpled grey hair stood up above his forehead like the crest of an angry bird, and the leather-brown of his veined cheeks was blotched with red. Charity knew that those red spots were the signs of a coming explosion.

Suddenly he said: "Where's supper? Has Verena Marsh slipped up again on her soda-biscuits?"

Charity threw a startled glance at him. "I

presume she's waiting for Mr. Harney."

"Mr. Harney, is she? She'd better dish up, then. He ain't coming." He stood up, walked to the door, and called out, in the pitch necessary to penetrate the old woman's tympanum: "Get along with the supper, Verena."

Charity was trembling with apprehension. Something had happened — she was sure of it now — and Mr. Royall knew what it was. But not for the world would she have gratified him by showing her anxiety. She took her usual place, and he seated himself opposite, and poured out a strong cup of tea before passing her the tea-pot. Verena brought some scrambled eggs, and he piled his plate with them. "Ain't you going to take any?" he asked. Charity roused herself and began to eat.

The tone with which Mr. Royall had said "He's not coming" seemed to her full of an ominous satisfaction. She saw that he had suddenly begun to hate Lucius Harney, and guessed herself to be the cause of this change of feeling. But she had no means of finding out whether some act of hostility on his part had made the young man stay away, or whether he simply wished to avoid seeing her again after their drive back from the brown house. She ate her supper with a studied show of indifference, but she knew that Mr. Royall was watching her and that her agitation did not escape him.

After supper she went up to her room. She heard Mr. Royall cross the passage, and presently the sounds below her window showed that he had returned to the porch. She seated herself on her bed and began to struggle against the desire to go down and ask him what had happened. "I'd rather die than to do it," she muttered to herself. With a word he could have relieved her uncertainty: but never would she gratify him by saying it.

She rose and leaned out of the window. The twilight had deepened into night, and she watched the frail curve of the young moon dropping to the edge of the hills. Through the darkness she saw one or two figures moving down the road; but the evening was too cold for loitering, and presently the strollers disappeared. Lamps were beginning to show here and there in the windows. A bar of light brought out the whiteness of a clump of lilies in the Hawes's yard: and farther down the street Carrick Fry's Rochester lamp cast its bold illumination on the rustic flower-tub in the middle of his grass-plot.

For a long time she continued to lean in the window. But a fever of unrest consumed her, and finally she went downstairs, took her hat from its hook, and swung out of the house. Mr. Royall sat on the porch,

Verena beside him, her old hands crossed on her patched skirt. As Charity went down the steps Mr. Royall called after her: "Where you going?" She could easily have answered: "To Orma's," or "Down to the Targatts' "; and either answer might have been true, for she had no purpose. But she swept on in silence, determined not to recognize his right to question her.

At the gate she paused and looked up and down the road. The darkness drew her, and she thought of climbing the hill and plunging into the depths of the larchwood above the pasture. Then she glanced irresolutely along the street, and as she did so a gleam appeared through the spruces at Miss Hatchard's gate. Lucius Harney was there, then — he had not gone down to Hepburn with Mr. Miles, as she had at first imagined. But where had he taken his evening meal, and what had caused him to stay away from Mr. Royall's? The light was positive proof of his presence, for Miss Hatchard's servants were away on a holiday, and her farmer's wife came only in the mornings, to make the young man's bed and prepare his coffee. Beside that lamp he was doubtless sitting at this moment. To know the truth Charity had only to walk half the length of the village, and knock at the lighted window. She hesitated a minute or two longer, and then turned toward Miss Hatchard's.

She walked quickly, straining her eyes to detect anyone who might be coming along the street; and before reaching the Frys' she crossed over to avoid the light from their window. Whenever she was unhappy she felt herself at bay against a pitiless world, and a kind of animal secretiveness possessed her. But the street was empty, and she passed unnoticed through the gate and up the path to the house. Its white front glimmered indistinctly through the trees, showing only one oblong of light on the lower floor. She had supposed that the lamp was in Miss Hatchard's sitting-room; but she now saw that it shone through a window at the farther corner of the house. She did not know the room to which this window belonged, and she paused under the trees, checked by a sense of strangeness. Then she moved on, treading softly on the short grass, and keeping so close to the house that whoever was in the room, even if roused by her approach, would not be able to see her.

The window opened on a narrow verandah with a trellised arch. She leaned close to the trellis, and parting the sprays of clematis that covered it looked into a corner of the room. She saw the foot of a mahogany bed, an engraving on the wall, a washstand on which a towel had been tossed, and one end of the green-covered table which held the lamp. Half of the lamp-shade projected into her field of vision, and just under it two smooth sunburnt hands, one holding a pencil and the other a ruler, were moving to and fro over a drawing-board.

Her heart jumped and then stood still. He was there, a few feet away; and while her soul was tossing on seas of woe he had been quietly sitting at his drawing-board. The sight of those two hands, moving with their usual skill and precision, woke her out of her dream. Her eyes were opened to the disproportion between what she had felt and the cause of her agitation; and she was turning away from the window when one hand abruptly pushed aside the drawing-board and the other flung down the pencil.

Charity had often noticed Harney's loving care of his drawings, and the neatness and method with which he carried on and con-cluded each task. The impatient sweeping aside of the drawing-board seemed to reveal a new mood. The gesture suggested sudden discouragement, or distaste for his work and she wondered if he too were agitated by secret perplexities. Her impulse of flight was checked; she stepped up on the veran-dah and looked into the room.

Harney had put his elbows on the table and was resting his chin on his locked hands. He had taken off his coat and waistcoat, and unbuttoned the low collar of his flannel shirt; she saw the vigourous lines of his young throat, and the root of the muscles where they joined the chest. He sat staring straight ahead of him, a look of weariness and self-disgust on his face: it was almost as if he had been gazing at a distorted reflection of his own features. For a moment Charity looked at him with a kind of terror, as if he had been a stranger under familiar lineaments; then she glanced past him and saw on the floor an open portmanteau half full of clothes. She understood that he was preparing to leave, and that he had probably decided to go without seeing her. She saw that the decision, from whatever cause it was taken, had disturbed him deeply; and she immediately concluded that his change of plan was due to some surreptitious interference of Mr. Royall's. All her old resentments and rebellions flamed up, confusedly mingled with the yearning roused by Harney's nearness. Only a few hours earlier she had felt secure in his comprehending pity; now she was flung back on herself, doubly alone after that moment of communion.

Harney was still unaware of her presence. He sat without moving, moodily staring before him at the same spot in the wall-paper. He had not even had the energy to finish his packing, and his clothes and papers lay on the floor about the portmanteau. Presently he unlocked his clasped hands and stood up; and Charity, drawing back hastily, sank down on the step of the verandah. The night was so dark that there was not much chance of his seeing her unless he opened the window and before that she would have time to slip away and be lost in the shadow of the trees. He stood for a minute or two looking around the room with the same expression of self-disgust, as if he hated himself and everything about him; then he sat down again at the table, drew a few more strokes, and threw his pencil aside. Finally he walked across the floor, kicking the portmanteau out of his way, and lay down on the bed, folding his arms under his head, and staring up morosely at the ceiling. Just so, Charity had seen him at her side on the grass or the pine-needles, his eyes fixed on the sky, and pleasure flashing over his face like the flickers of sun the branches shed on it. But now the face was so changed that she hardly knew it; and grief at his grief gathered in her throat, rose to her eyes and ran over.

She continued to crouch on the steps, holding her breath and stiffening herself into complete immobility. One motion of her hand, one tap on the pane, and she could picture the sudden change in his face. In

every pulse of her rigid body she was aware
of the welcome his eyes and lips would give
her; but something kept her from moving.
It was not the fear of any sanction, human
or heavenly; she had never in her life been
afraid. It was simply that she had suddenly
understood what would happen if she went
in. It was the thing that *did* happen between young men and girls, and that North
Dormer ignored in public and snickered
over on the sly. It was what Miss Hatchard
was still ignorant of, but every girl of Charity's class knew about before she left
school. It was what had happened to Ally
Hawes's sister Julia, and had ended in her
going to Nettleton, and in people's never
mentioning her name.

It did not, of course, always end so sen-
sationally; nor, perhaps, on the whole, so
untragically. Charity had always suspected
that the shunned Julia's fate might have
its compensations. There were others,
worse endings that the village knew of,
mean, miserable, unconfessed; other lives
that went on drearily, without visible
change, in the same cramped setting of
hypocrisy. But these were not the reasons
that held her back. Since the day before,
she had known exactly what she would feel
if Harney should take her in his arms: the
melting of palm into palm and mouth on
mouth, and the long flame burning her

from head to foot. But mixed with this feeling was another: the wondering pride in his liking for her, the startled softness that his sympathy had put into her heart. Sometimes, when her youth flushed up in her, she had imagined yielding like other girls to furtive caresses in the twilight; but she could not so cheapen herself to Harney. She did not know why he was going; but since he was going she felt she must do nothing to deface the image of her that he carried away. If he wanted her he must seek her: he must not be surprised into taking her as girls like Julia Hawes were taken. . . .

No sound came from the sleeping village, and in the deep darkness of the garden she heard now and then a secret rustle of branches, as though some night-bird brushed them. Once a footfall passed the gate, and she shrank back into her corner; but the steps died away and left a profounder quiet. Her eyes were still on Harney's tormented face: she felt she could not move till he moved. But she was beginning to grow numb from her constrained position, and at times her thoughts were so indistinct that she seemed to be held there only by a vague weight of weariness.

A long time passed in this strange vigil. Harney still lay on the bed, motionless and with fixed eyes, as though following his vision to its bitter end. At last he stirred and changed his attitude slightly, and Charity's heart began to tremble. But he only flung out his arms and sank back into his former position. With a deep sigh he tossed the hair from his forehead; then his whole body relaxed, his head turned sideways on the pillow, and she saw that he had fallen asleep. The sweet expression came back to his lips, and the haggardness faded from his face, leaving it as fresh as a boy's.

She rose and crept away.

VIII

She had lost the sense of time, and did not know how late it was till she came out into the street and saw that all the windows were dark between Miss Hatchard's and the Royall house.

As she passed from under the black pall of the Norway spruces she fancied she saw two figures in the shade about the duck-pond. She drew back and watched; but nothing moved, and she had stared so long into the lamp-lit room that the darkness confused her, and she thought she must have been mistaken.

She walked on, wondering whether Mr. Royall was still on the porch. In her exalted mood she did not greatly care whether he was waiting for her or not: she seemed to be floating high over life, on a great cloud of misery beneath which everyday realities had dwindled to mere specks in space. But the porch was empty, Mr. Royall's hat hung on its peg in the passage, and the kitchen lamp had been left to light her to bed. She took it and went up.

The morning hours of the next day

dragged by without incident. Charity had imagined that, in some way or other, she would learn whether Harney had already left; but Verena's deafness prevented her being a source of news, and no one came to the house who could bring enlightenment.

Mr. Royall went out early, and did not return till Verena had set the table for the midday meal. When he came in he went straight to the kitchen and shouted to the old woman: "Ready for dinner —" then he turned into the dining-room, where Charity was already seated. Harney's plate was in its usual place, but Mr. Royall offered no explanation of his absence, and Charity asked none. The feverish exaltation of the night before had dropped, and she said to herself that he had gone away, indifferently, almost callously, and that now her life would lapse again into the narrow rut out of which he had lifted it. For a moment she was inclined to sneer at herself for not having used the arts that might have kept him.

She sat at table till the meal was over, lest Mr. Royall should remark on her leaving; but when he stood up she rose also, without waiting to help Verena. She had her foot on the stairs when he called to her to come back.

"I've got a headache. I'm going up to lie down."

"I want you should come in here first; I've got something to say to you."

She was sure from his tone that in a moment she would learn what every nerve in her ached to know; but as she turned back she made a last effort of indifference.

Mr. Royall stood in the middle of the office, his thick eyebrows beetling, his lower jaw trembling a little. At first she thought he had been drinking; then she saw that he was sober, but stirred by a deep and stern emotion totally unlike his usual transient angers. And suddenly she understood that, until then, she had never really noticed him or thought about him. Except on the occasion of his one offense he had been to her merely the person who is always there, the unquestioned central fact of life, as inevitable but as uninteresting as North Dormer itself, or any of the other conditions fate had laid on her. Even then she had regarded him only in relation to herself, and had never speculated as to his own feelings, beyond instinctively concluding that he would not trouble her again in the same way. But now she began to wonder what he was really like.

He had grasped the back of his chair with both hands, and stood looking hard at her. At length he said: "Charity, for once let's you and me talk together like friends."

Instantly she felt that something had happened, and that he held her in his hand.

"Where is Mr. Harney? Why hasn't he come back? Have you sent him away?" she broke out, without knowing what she was saying.

The change in Mr. Royall frightened her. All the blood seemed to leave his veins and against his swarthy pallor the deep lines in his face looked black.

"Didn't he have time to answer some of those questions last night? You was with him long enough!" he said.

Charity stood speechless. The taunt was so unrelated to what had been happening in her soul that she hardly understood it. But the instinct of self-defense awoke in her.

"Who says I was with him last night?"

"The whole place is saying it by now."

"Then it was you that put the lie into their mouths. — Oh, how I've always hated you!" she cried.

She had expected a retort in kind, and it startled her to hear her exclamation sounding on through silence.

"Yes, I know," Mr. Royall said slowly. "But that ain't going to help us much now."

"It helps me not to care a straw what lies you tell about me!"

"If they're lies, they're not my lies: my Bible oath on that, Charity. I didn't know where you were: I wasn't out of this house last night."

She made no answer and he went on: "Is it a lie that you were seen coming out of Miss Hatchard's nigh onto midnight?"

She straightened herself with a laugh, all her reckless insolence recovered. "I didn't look to see what time it was."

"You lost girl . . . you . . . you . . . Oh, my God, why did you tell me?" he broke out, dropping into his chair, his head bowed down like an old man's.

Charity's self-possession had returned with the sense of her danger. "Do you suppose I'd take the trouble to lie to *you?* Who are you, anyhow, to ask me where I go to when I go out at night?"

Mr. Royall lifted his head and looked at her. His face had grown quiet and almost gentle, as she remembered seeing it sometimes when she was a little girl, before Mrs. Royall died.

"Don't let's go on like this, Charity. It can't do any good to either of us. You were seen going into that fellow's house . . . you were seen coming out of it. . . . I've watched this thing coming, and I've tried to stop it. As God sees me, I have. . . ."

"Ah, it *was* you, then? I knew it was you that sent him away!"

He looked at her in surprise. "Didn't he tell you so? I thought he understood." He spoke slowly, with difficult pauses, "I didn't name you to him: I'd have cut my hand off sooner. I just told him I couldn't spare the horse any longer; and that the cooking was getting too heavy for Verena. I guess he's the kind that's heard the same thing before. Anyhow, he took it quietly enough. He said his job here was about done, anyhow; and there didn't another word pass between us. . . . If he told you otherwise he told you an untruth."

Charity listened in a cold trance of anger. It was nothing to her what the village said . . . but all this fingering of her dreams!

"I've told you he didn't tell me anything. I didn't speak with him last night."

"You didn't speak with him?"

"No. . . . It's not that I care what any of you say . . . but you may as well know. Things ain't between us the way you think . . . and the other people in this place. He was kind to me; he was my friend; and all of a sudden he stopped coming, and I knew it was you that done it — *you!*" All her unreconciled memory of the past flamed out at him. "So I went there last night to find out what you'd said to him: that's all."

Mr. Royall drew a heavy breath. "But, then — if he wasn't there, what were you doing there all that time? — Charity, for pity's sake, tell me. I've got to know, to stop their talking."

This pathetic abdication of all authority over her did not move her: she could feel only the outrage of his interference.

"Can't you see that I don't care what anybody says? It's true I went there to see him; and he was in his room, and I stood outside for ever so long and watched him; but I dursn't go in for fear he'd think I'd come after him. . . ." She felt her voice breaking, and gathered it up in a last defiance. "As long as I live I'll never forgive you!" she cried.

Mr. Royall made no answer. He sat and pondered with sunken head, his veined hands clasped about the arms of his chair. Age seemed to have come down on him as winter comes on the hills after a storm. At length he looked up.

"Charity, you say you don't care; but you're the proudest girl I know, and the last to want people to talk against you. You know there's always eyes watching you: you're handsomer and smarter than the rest, and that's enough. But till lately you've never given them a chance. Now they've got it, and they're going to use it. I believe what you say, but they won't. . . . It was Mrs. Tom Fry seen you going in . . . and two or three of them watched for you to come out again. . . . You've been with the fellow all day long every day since he come here . . . and I'm a lawyer, and I know how hard slander dies." He paused, but she stood motionless, without giving him any sign of acquiescence or even of attention. "He's a pleasant fellow to talk to — I liked having him here myself. The young men up here ain't had his chances. But there's one thing as old as the hills and as plain as daylight: if he'd wanted you the right way he'd have said so."

Charity did not speak. It seemed to her that nothing could exceed the bitterness of hearing such words from such lips.

Mr. Royall rose from his seat. "See here, Charity Royall: I had a shameful thought once, and you've made me pay for it. Isn't that score pretty near wiped out? . . . There's a streak in me I ain't always master of; but I've always acted straight to you but that once. And you've known I would — you've trusted me. For all your sneers and your mockery you've always known I loved you the way a man loves a decent woman. I'm a good many years older than you, but I'm head and shoulders above this place and everybody in it, and you know that too. I slipped up once, but that's no reason for not starting again. If you'll come with me I'll do it. If you'll marry me we'll leave here and settle in some big town, where there's men, and business, and things doing. It's not too late for me to find an opening. . . . I can see it by the way folks treat me when I go down to Hepburn or Nettleton. . . ."

Charity made no movement. Nothing in

his appeal reached her heart, and she thought only of words to wound and wither. But a growing lassitude restrained her. What did anything matter that he was saying? She saw the old life closing in on her, and hardly heeded his fanciful picture of renewal.

"Charity — Charity — say you'll do it," she heard him urge, all his lost years and wasted passion in his voice.

"Oh, what's the use of all this? When I leave here it won't be with you."

She moved toward the door as she spoke, and he stood up and placed himself between her and the threshold. He seemed suddenly tall and strong, as though the extremity of his humiliation had given him new vigour.

"That's all, is it? It's not much." He leaned against the door, so towering and powerful that he seemed to fill the narrow room. "Well, then — look here. . . . You're right: I've no claim on you — why should you look at a broken man like me? You want the other fellow . . . and I don't blame you. You picked out the best when you seen it . . . well, that was always my way." He fixed his stern eyes on her, and she had the sense that the struggle within him was at its highest. "Do you want him to marry you?" he asked.

They stood and looked at each other for

a long moment, eye to eye, with the terrible equality of courage that sometimes made her feel as if she had his blood in her veins.

"Do you want him to — say? I'll have him here in an hour if you do. I ain't been in the law thirty years for nothing. He's hired Carrick Fry's team to take him to Hepburn, but he ain't going to start for another hour. And I can put things to him so he won't be long deciding. . . . He's soft: I could see that. I don't say you won't be sorry afterward — but, by God, I'll give you the chance to be, if you say so."

She heard him out in silence, too remote from all he was feeling and saying for any sally of scorn to relieve her. As she listened, there flitted through her mind the vision of Liff Hyatt's muddy boot coming down on the white bramble-flowers. The same thing had happened now; something transient and exquisite had flowered in her, and she had stood by and seen it trampled to earth. While the thought passed through her she was aware of Mr. Royall, still leaning against the door, but crestfallen, diminished, as though her silence were the answer he most dreaded.

"I don't want any chance you can give me: I'm glad he's going away," she said.

He kept his place a moment longer, his hand on the door-knob. "Charity!" he pleaded. She made no answer, and he turned the knob and went out. She heard him fumble with the latch of the front door, and saw him walk down the steps. He passed out of the gate, and his figure, stooping and heavy, receded slowly up the street.

For a while she remained where he had left her. She was still trembling with the humiliation of his last words, which rang so loud in her ears that it seemed as though they must echo through the village, proclaiming her a creature to lend herself to such vile suggestions. Her shame weighed on her like a physical oppression: the roof and walls seemed to be closing in on her, and she was seized by the impulse to get away, under the open sky, where there would be room to breathe. She went to the front door, and as she did so Lucius Harney opened it.

He looked graver and less confident than usual, and for a moment or two neither of them spoke. Then he held out his hand. "Are you going out?" he asked. "May I come in?"

Her heart was beating so violently that she was afraid to speak, and stood looking at him with tear-dilated eyes; then she became aware of what her silence must betray, and said quickly: "Yes: come in."

She led the way into the dining-room, and they sat down on opposite sides of the table, the cruet-stand and japanned bread-basket between them. Harney had laid his straw hat on the table, and as he sat there, in his easy-looking summer clothes, a brown tie knotted under his flannel collar, and his smooth brown hair brushed back from his forehead, she pictured him, as she had seen him the night before, lying on his bed, with the tossed locks falling into his eyes, and his bare throat rising out of his unbuttoned shirt. He had never seemed so remote as at the moment when that vision flashed through her mind.

"I'm so sorry it's good-bye: I suppose you know I'm leaving," he began, abruptly and awkwardly; she guessed that he was wondering how much she knew of his reason for going.

"I presume you found your work was over quicker than what you expected," she said.

"Well, yes — that is, no: there are plenty of things I should have liked to do. But my holiday's limited; and now that Mr. Royall needs the horse for himself it's rather difficult to find means of getting about."

"There ain't any too many teams for hire around here," she acquiesced; and there was another silence.

"These days here have been — awfully pleasant: I wanted to thank you for making them so," he continued, his colour rising.

She could not think of any reply, and he

went on: "You've been wonderfully kind to me, and I wanted to tell you. . . . I wish I could think of you as happier, less lonely. . . . Things are sure to change for you by and by. . . ."

"Things don't change at North Dormer: people just get used to them."

The answer seemed to break up the order of his prearranged consolations, and he sat looking at her uncertainly. Then he said, with his sweet smile: "That's not true of you. It can't be."

The smile was like a knife-thrust through her heart: everything in her began to tremble and break loose. She felt her tears run over, and stood up.

"Well, good-bye," she said.

She was aware of his taking her hand, and of feeling that his touch was lifeless.

"Good-bye." He turned away, and stopped on the threshold. "You'll say good-bye for me to Verena?"

She heard the closing of the outer door and the sound of his quick tread along the path. The latch of the gate clicked after him.

The next morning when she arose in the cold dawn and opened her shutters she saw a freckled boy standing on the other side of the road and looking up at her. He was a boy from a farm three or four miles down the Creston road, and she wondered what he was doing there at that hour, and why he looked so hard at her window. When he saw her he crossed over and leaned against the gate unconcernedly. There was no one stirring in the house, and she threw a shawl over her nightgown and ran down and let herself out. By the time she reached the gate the boy was sauntering down the road, whistling carelessly; but she saw that a letter had been thrust between the slats and the crossbar of the gate. She took it out and hastened back to her room.

The envelope bore her name, and inside was a leaf torn from a pocket-diary.

DEAR CHARITY:

I can't go away like this. I am staying for a few days at Creston River. Will you come down and meet me at Creston pool? I will wait for you till evening.

IX

Charity sat before the mirror trying on a hat which Ally Hawes, with much secrecy, had trimmed for her. It was of white straw, with a drooping brim and cherry-coloured lining that made her face glow like the inside of the shell on the parlour mantelpiece.

She propped the square of looking-glass against Mr. Royall's black leather Bible, steadying it in front with a white stone on which a view of the Brooklyn Bridge was painted; and she sat before her reflection, bending the brim this way and that, while Ally Hawes's pale face looked over her shoulder like the ghost of wasted opportunities.

"I look awful, don't I?" she said at last with a happy sigh.

Ally smiled and took back the hat. "I'll stitch the roses on right here, so's you can put it away at once."

Charity laughed, and ran her fingers through her rough dark hair. She knew that Harney liked to see its reddish edges ruffled about her forehead and breaking into little rings at the nape. She sat down on her bed and watched Ally stoop over the hat with a careful frown.

"Don't you ever feel like going down to Nettleton for a day?" she asked.

Ally shook her head without looking up. "No, I always remember that awful time I went down with Julia — to that doctor's."

"Oh, Ally —"

"I can't help it. The house is on the corner of Wing Street and Lake Avenue. The trolley from the station goes right by it, and the day the minister took us down to see those pictures I recognized it right off, and couldn't seem to see anything else. There's a big black sign with gold letters all across the front — 'Private Consultations.' She came as near as anything to dying. . . ."

"Poor Julia!" Charity sighed from the height of her purity and her security. She had a friend whom she trusted and who respected her. She was going with him to spend the next day — the Fourth of July — at Nettleton. Whose business was it but hers, and what was the harm? The pity of it was that girls like Julia did not know how to choose, and to keep bad fellows at a distance. . . . Charity slipped down from the bed, and stretched out her hands.

"Is it sewed? Let me try it on again." She put the hat on, and smiled at her image. The thought of Julia had vanished. . . .

The next morning she was up before dawn, and saw the yellow sunrise broaden behind the hills, and the silvery luster preceding a hot day tremble across the sleeping fields.

Her plans had been made with great care. She had announced that she was going down to the Band of Hope picnic at Hepburn, and as no one else from North Dormer intended to venture so far it was not likely that her absence from the festivity would be reported. Besides, if it were she would not greatly care. She was determined to assert her independence, and if she stooped to fib about the Hepburn picnic it was chiefly from the secretive instinct that made her dread the profanation of her happiness. Whenever she was with Lucius Harney she would have liked some impenetrable mountain mist to hide her.

It was arranged that she should walk to a point of the Creston road where Harney was to pick her up and drive her across the hills to Hepburn in time for the nine-thirty train to Nettleton. Harney at first had been rather lukewarm about the trip. He declared himself ready to take her to Nettleton, but urged her not to go on the Fourth of July on account of the crowds, the probable lateness of the trains, the difficulty of her getting back before night; but her evident disappointment caused him to give way, and even to affect a faint enthusiasm for the adventure. She understood why he was not more eager: he must have seen sights beside which even a Fourth of July at Nettleton would seem tame. But she had never seen anything; and a great longing possessed her to walk the streets of a big town on a holiday, clinging to his arm and jostled by idle crowds in their best clothes. The only cloud on the prospect was the fact that the shops would be closed; but she hoped he would take her back another day, when they were open.

She started out unnoticed in the early sunlight, slipping through the kitchen while Verena bent above the stove. To avoid attracting notice, she carried her new hat carefully wrapped up, and had thrown a long grey veil of Mrs. Royall's over the new white muslin dress which Ally's clever fingers had made for her. All of the ten dollars Mr. Royall had given her, and a part of her own savings as well, had been spent on renewing her wardrobe; and when Harney jumped out of the buggy to meet her she read her reward in his eyes.

The freckled boy who had brought her the note two weeks earlier was to wait with the buggy at Hepburn till their return. He perched at Charity's feet, his legs dangling between the wheels, and they could not say much because of his presence. But it did not greatly matter, for their past was now rich enough to have given them a private language; and with the long day stretching before them like the blue distance beyond the hills there was a delicate pleasure in postponement.

When Charity, in response to Harney's message, had gone to meet him at the Creston pool her heart had been so full of mortification and anger that his first words might easily have estranged her. But it happened that he had found the right word, which was one of simple friendship. His tone had instantly justified her, and put her guardian in the wrong. He had made no allusion to what had passed between Mr. Royall and himself, but had simply let it appear that he had left because means of conveyance were hard to find at North Dormer, and because Creston River was a more convenient centre. He told her that he had hired by the week the buggy of the freckled boy's father, who served as livery-stable keeper to one or two melancholy summer boardinghouses on Creston Lake, and had discovered, within driving distance, a number of houses worthy of his pencil; and he said that he could not, while he was in the neighbourhood, give up the pleasure of seeing her as often as possible.

When they took leave of each other she

promised to continue to be his guide; and during the fortnight which followed they roamed the hills in happy comradeship. In most of the village friendships between youths and maidens lack of conversation was made up for by tentative fondling; but Harney, except when he had tried to comfort her in her trouble on their way back from the Hyatts', had never put his arm about her, or sought to betray her into any sudden caress. It seemed to be enough for him to breathe her nearness like a flower's; and since his pleasure at being with her, and his sense of her youth and her grace, perpetually shone in his eyes and softened the inflection of his voice, his reserve did not suggest coldness, but the deference due to a girl of his own class.

The buggy was drawn by an old trotter who whirled them along so briskly that the pace created a little breeze; but when they reached Hepburn the full heat of the airless morning descended on them. At the railway station the platform was packed with a sweltering throng, and they took refuge in the waiting-room, where there was another throng, already dejected by the heat and the long waiting for retarded trains. Pale mothers were struggling with fretful babies, or trying to keep their older offspring from the fascination of the track; girls and their "fellows" were giggling and shoving, and passing about candy in sticky bags, and older men, collarless and perspiring, were shifting heavy children from one arm to the other, and keeping a haggard eye on the scattered members of their families.

At last the train rumbled in, and engulfed the waiting multitude. Harney swept Charity up on to the first car and they captured a bench for two, and sat in happy isolation while the train swayed and roared along through rich fields and languid tree-clumps. The haze of the morning had become a sort of clear tremour over everything, like the colourless vibration about a flame; and the opulent landscape seemed to droop under it. But to Charity the heat was a stimulant: it enveloped the whole world in the same glow that burned at her heart. Now and then a lurch of the train flung her against Harney, and through her thin muslin she felt the touch of his sleeve. She steadied herself, their eyes met, and the flaming breath of the day seemed to enclose them.

The train roared into the Nettleton station, the descending mob caught them on its tide, and they were swept out into a vague dusty square thronged with seedy "hacks" and long curtained omnibuses drawn by horses with tasselled fly-nets over their withers, who stood swinging their depressed heads drearily from side to side.

A mob of 'bus and hack drivers were

shouting "To the Eagle House," "To the Washington House," "This way to the Lake," "Just starting for Greytop"; and through their yells came the popping of fire-crackers, the explosion of torpedoes, the banging of toy-guns, and the crash of a firemen's band trying to play the Merry Widow while they were being packed into a waggonette streaming with bunting.

The ramshackle wooden hotels about the square were all hung with flags and paper lanterns, and as Harney and Charity turned into the main street, with its brick and granite business blocks crowding out the old low-storied shops, and its towering poles strung with innumerable wires that seemed to tremble and buzz in the heat, they saw the double line of flags and lanterns tapering away gaily to the park at the other end of the perspective. The noise and colour of this holiday vision seemed to transform Nettleton into a metropolis. Charity could not believe that Springfield or even Boston had anything grander to show, and she wondered if, at this very moment, Annabel Balch, on the arm of as brilliant a young man, were threading her way through scenes as resplendent.

"Where shall we go first?" Harney asked; but as she turned her happy eyes on him he guessed the answer and said: "We'll take a look around, shall we?"

The street swarmed with their fellow-travellers, with other excursionists arriving from other directions, with Nettleton's own population, and with the mill-hands trooping in from the factories on the Creston. The shops were closed, but one would scarcely have noticed it, so numerous were the glass doors swinging open on saloons, on restaurants, on drug-stores gushing from every soda-water tap, on fruit and confectionery shops stacked with strawberry-cake, cocoanut drops, trays of glistening molasses candy, boxes of caramels and chewing-gum, baskets of sodden strawberries, and dangling branches of bananas. Outside of some of the doors were trestles with banked-up oranges and apples, spotted pears and dusty raspberries; and the air reeked with the smell of fruit and stale coffee, beer and sarsaparilla and fried potatoes.

Even the shops that were closed offered, through wide expanses of plate-glass, hints of hidden riches. In some, waves of silk and ribbon broke over shores of imitation moss from which ravishing hats rose like tropical orchids. In others, the pink throats of gramophones opened their giant convolutions in a soundless chorus; or bicycles shining in neat ranks seemed to await the signal of an invisible starter; or tiers of fancy-goods in leatherette and paste and celluloid dangled their insidious graces; and, in one vast bay that seemed to project them into exciting contact with the public, wax ladies in daring dresses chatted elegantly, or, with gestures intimate yet blameless, pointed to their pink corsets and transparent hosiery.

Presently Harney found that his watch had stopped, and turned in at a small jeweller's shop which chanced to be still open. While the watch was being examined Charity leaned over the glass counter where, on a background of dark blue velvet, pins, rings and brooches glittered like the moon and stars. She had never seen jewellery so near by, and she longed to lift the glass lid and plunge her hand among the shining treasures. But already Harney's watch was repaired, and he laid his hand on her arm and drew her from her dream.

"Which do you like best?" he asked leaning over the counter at her side.

"I don't know. . . ." She pointed to a gold lily of the valley with white flowers.

"Don't you think the blue pin's better?" he suggested, and immediately she saw that the lily of the valley was mere trumpery compared to the small round stone, blue as a mountain lake, with little sparks of light all round it. She coloured at her want of discrimination.

"It's so lovely I guess I was afraid to look at it," she said.

He laughed, and they went out of the shop; but a few steps away he exclaimed: "Oh, by Jove, I forgot something," and turned back and left her in the crowd. She stood staring down a row of pink gramophone throats till he rejoined her and slipped his arm through hers.

"You mustn't be afraid of looking at the blue pin any longer, because it belongs to you," he said; and she felt a little box being pressed into her hand. Her heart gave a leap of joy, but it reached her lips only in a shy stammer. She remembered other girls whom she had heard planning to extract presents from their fellows, and was seized with a sudden dread lest Harney should have imagined that she had leaned over the pretty things in the glass case in the hope of having one given to her. . . .

A little farther down the street they turned in at a glass doorway opening on a shining hall with a mahogany staircase, and brass cages in its corners. "We must have something to eat," Harney said; and the next moment Charity found herself in a dressing-room all looking-glass and lustrous surfaces, where a party of showy-looking girls were dabbing on powder and straightening immense plumed hats. When they had gone she took courage to bathe her hot face in one of the marble basins, and to straighten her own hat-brim, which the parasols of the crowd had indented. The dresses in the shops had so impressed her that she scarcely dared look at her reflection; but when she did so, the glow of her face under her cherry-coloured hat, and the curve of her young shoulders through the transparent muslin, restored her courage; and when she had taken the blue brooch from its box and pinned it on her bosom she walked toward the restaurant with her head high, as if she had always strolled through tessellated halls beside young men in flannels.

Her spirit sank a little at the sight of the slim-waisted waitresses in black, with bewitching mobcaps on their haughty heads, who were moving disdainfully between the tables. "Not f'r another hour," one of them dropped to Harney in passing; and he stood doubtfully glancing about him.

"Oh, well, we can't stay sweltering here," he decided; "let's try somewhere else —" and with a sense of relief Charity followed him from that scene of inhospitable splendour.

That "somewhere else" turned out — after more hot tramping, and several failures — to be, of all things, a little open-air place in a back street that called itself a French restaurant, and consisted in two or three rickety tables under a scarlet-runner, between a patch of zinnias and petunias and a big elm bending over from the next yard. Here they lunched on queerly flavoured things, while Harney, leaning back in a crippled rocking-chair, smoked cigarettes between the courses and poured into Charity's glass a pale yellow wine which he said was the very same one drank in just such jolly places in France.

Charity did not think the wine as good as sarsaparilla, but she sipped a mouthful for the pleasure of doing what he did, and of fancying herself alone with him in foreign countries. The illusion was increased by their being served by a deep-bosomed woman with smooth hair and a pleasant laugh, who talked to Harney in unintelligible words, and seemed amazed and overjoyed at his answering her in kind. At the other tables other people sat, mill-hands probably, homely but pleasant looking, who spoke the same shrill jargon, and looked at Harney and Charity with friendly eyes; and between the table-legs a poodle with bald patches and pink eyes nosed about for scraps, and sat up on his hind legs absurdly.

Harney showed no inclination to move, for hot as their corner was, it was at least shaded and quiet; and, from the main thoroughfares came the clanging of trolleys, the incessant popping of torpedoes, the jingle of street-organs, the bawling of megaphone men and the loud murmur of increasing crowds. He leaned back, smoking his cigar, patting the dog, and stirring the coffee that steamed in their chipped cups. "It's the real thing, you know," he explained; and Charity hastily revised her previous conception of the beverage.

They had made no plans for the rest of the day, and when Harney asked her what she wanted to do next she was too bewildered by rich possibilities to find an answer. Finally she confessed that she longed to go to the Lake, where she had not been taken on her former visit, and when he answered, "Oh, there's time for that — it will be pleasanter later," she suggested seeing some pictures like the ones Mr. Miles had taken her to. She thought Harney looked a little disconcerted; but he passed his fine handkerchief over his warm brow, said gaily, "Come along, then," and rose with a last pat for the pink-eyed dog.

Mr. Miles's pictures had been shown in an austere Y.M.C.A. hall, with white walls and an organ; but Harney led Charity to a glittering place — everything she saw seemed to glitter — where they passed, between immense pictures of yellow-haired beauties stabbing villains in evening dress, into a velvet-curtained auditorium packed with spectators to the last limit of compression. After that, for a while, everything was merged in her brain in swimming circles of heat and blinding alternations of light and darkness. All the world has to show seemed to pass before her in a chaos of palms and minarets, charging cavalry regiments, roaring lions, comic policemen and scowling murderers; and the crowd around her, the hundreds of hot sallow candy-munching faces, young, old, middle-aged, but all kindled with the same contagious excitement, became part of the spectacle, and danced on the screen with the rest.

Presently the thought of the cool trolley-run to the Lake grew irresistible, and they struggled out of the theatre. As they stood on the pavement, Harney pale with the heat, and even Charity a little confused by it, a young man drove by in an electric run-about with a calico band bearing the words: "Ten dollars to take you round the Lake." Before Charity knew what was happening, Harney had waved a hand, and they were climbing in. "Say, for twenny-five I'll run you out to see the ball-game and back," the driver proposed with an insinuating grin; but Charity said quickly: "Oh, I'd rather go rowing on the Lake." The street was so thronged that progress was slow; but the glory of sitting in the little carriage while it wriggled its way between laden omnibuses and trolleys made the moments seem too short. "Next turn is Lake Avenue," the young man called out over his shoulder; and as they paused in the wake of a big omnibus groaning with Knights of Pythias in cocked hats and swords, Charity looked up and saw on the corner a brick house with a conspicuous black and gold sign across its front. "Dr. Merkle; Private Consultations at all hours. Lady Attendants," she read; and suddenly she remembered Ally Hawes's words: "The house was at the corner of Wing Street and Lake Avenue . . . there's a big black sign across the front. . . ." Through all the heat and the rapture a shiver of cold ran over her.

X

The Lake at last — a sheet of shining metal brooded over by drooping trees. Charity and Harney had secured a boat and, getting away from the wharves and the refreshment-booths, they drifted idly along, hugging the shadow of the shore. Where the sun struck the water its shafts flamed back blindingly at the heat-veiled sky; and the least shade was black by contrast. The Lake was so smooth that the reflection of the trees on its edge seemed enamelled on a solid surface; but gradually, as the sun declined, the water grew transparent, and Charity, leaning over, plunged her fascinated gaze into depths so clear that she saw the inverted tree-tops interwoven with the green growths of the bottom.

They rounded a point at the farther end of the Lake, and entering an inlet pushed their bow against a protruding tree-trunk. A green veil of willows overhung them. Beyond the trees, wheat-fields sparkled in the sun; and all along the horizon the clear hills throbbed with light. Charity leaned back in the stern, and Harney unshipped the oars and lay in the bottom of the boat without speaking.

Ever since their meeting at the Creston pool he had been subject to these brooding silences, which were as different as possible from the pauses when they ceased to speak because words were needless. At such times his face wore the expression she had seen on it when she had looked in at him from the darkness and again there came over her a sense of the mysterious distance between them; but usually his fits of abstraction were followed by bursts of gaiety that chased away the shadow before it chilled her.

She was still thinking of the ten dollars he had handed to the driver of the runabout. It had given them twenty minutes of pleasure, and it seemed unimaginable that anyone should be able to buy amusement at that rate. With ten dollars he might have bought her an engagement ring; she knew that Mrs. Tom Fry's, which came from Springfield, and had a diamond in it, had cost only eight seventy-five. But she did not know why the thought had occurred to her. Harney would never buy her an engagement ring: they were friends and comrades, but no more. He had been perfectly fair to her: he had never said a word to mislead her. She wondered what the girl was like whose hand was waiting for his ring. . . .

Boats were beginning to thicken on the Lake and the clang of incessantly arriving trolleys announced the return of the crowds from the ball-field. The shadows lengthened across the pearl-grey water and two white clouds near the sun were turning golden. On the opposite shore men were hammering hastily at a wooden scaffolding in a field. Charity asked what it was for.

"Why, the fireworks. I suppose there'll be a big show." Harney looked at her and a smile crept into his moody eyes. "Have you never seen any good fireworks?"

"Miss Hatchard always sends up lovely rockets on the Fourth," she answered doubtfully.

"Oh —" his contempt was unbounded. "I mean a big performance like this, illuminated boats, and all the rest."

She flushed at the picture. "Do they send them up from the Lake, too?"

"Rather. Didn't you notice that big raft we passed? It's wonderful to see the rockets completing their orbits down under one's feet." She said nothing, and he put the oars into the rowlocks. "If we stay we'd better go and pick up something to eat."

"But how can we get back afterwards?" she ventured, feeling it would break her heart if she missed it.

He consulted a time-table, found a ten o'clock train and reassured her. "The moon rises so late that it will be dark by eight, and we'll have over an hour of it."

Twilight fell, and lights began to show along the shore. The trolleys roaring out from Nettleton became great luminous serpents coiling in and out among the trees. The wooden eating-houses at the Lake's edge danced with lanterns, and the dusk echoed with laughter and shouts and the clumsy splashing of oars.

Harney and Charity had found a table in the corner of a balcony built over the Lake, and were patiently awaiting an unattainable chowder. Close under them the water lapped the piles, agitated by the evolutions of a little white steamboat trellised with coloured globes which was to run passengers up and down the Lake. It was already black with them as it sheered off on its first trip.

Suddenly Charity heard a woman's laugh behind her. The sound was familiar, and she turned to look. A band of showily dressed girls and dapper young men wearing badges of secret societies, with new straw hats tilted far back on their square-clipped hair, had invaded the balcony and were loudly clamouring for a table. The girl in the lead was the one who had laughed. She wore a large hat with a long white feather, and from under its brim her painted eyes looked at Charity with amused recognition.

"Say! if this ain't like Old Home Week," she remarked to the girl at her elbow; and giggles and glances passed between them. Charity knew at once that the girl with the white feather was Julia Hawes. She had lost her freshness, and the paint under her eyes made her face seem thinner; but her lips had the same lovely curve, and the same cold mocking smile, as if there were some secret absurdity in the person she was looking at, and she had instantly detected it.

Charity flushed to the forehead and looked away. She felt herself humiliated by Julia's sneer, and vexed that the mockery of such a creature should affect her. She trembled lest Harney should notice that the noisy troop had recognized her; but they found no table free, and passed on tumultuously.

Presently there was a soft rush through the air and a shower of silver fell from the blue evening sky. In another direction, pale Roman candles shot up singly through the trees, and a fire-haired rocket swept the horizon like a portent. Between these intermittent flashes the velvet curtains of the darkness were descending, and in the intervals of eclipse the voices of the crowds seemed to sink to smothered murmurs.

Charity and Harney, dispossessed by newcomers, were at length obliged to give up their table and struggle through the throng about the boat-landings. For a while there seemed no escape from the tide of late arrivals; but finally Harney secured the last two places on the stand from which the more privileged were to see the fireworks. The seats were at the end of a row, one above the other. Charity had taken off her hat to have an uninterrupted view; and whenever she leaned back to follow the curve of some dishevelled rocket she could feel Harney's knees against her head.

After a while the scattered fireworks ceased. A longer interval of darkness followed, and then the whole night broke into flower. From every point of the horizon, gold and silver arches sprang up and crossed each other, sky-orchards broke into blossom, shed their flaming petals and hung their branches with golden fruit; and all the while the air was filled with a soft supernatural hum, as though great birds were building their nests in those invisible tree-tops.

Now and then there came a lull, and a wave of moonlight swept the Lake. In a flash it revealed hundreds of boats, steel-dark against lustrous ripples; then it withdrew as if with a furling of vast translucent wings. Charity's heart throbbed with delight. It was as if all the latent beauty of things had been unveiled to her. She could not imagine that the world held anything more wonderful; but near her she heard someone say, "You wait till you see the set piece," and instantly her hopes took a fresh flight. At last, just as it was beginning to seem as though the whole arch of the sky were one great lid pressed against her dazzled eye-balls, and striking out of them continuous jets of jewelled light, the velvet darkness settled down again, and a murmur of expectation ran through the crowd.

"Now — now!" the same voice said excitedly; and Charity, grasping the hat on her knee, crushed it tight in the effort to restrain her rapture.

For a moment the night seemed to grow more impenetrably black; then a great picture stood out against it like a constellation. It was surmounted by a golden scroll bearing the inscription, "Washington crossing the Delaware," and across a flood of motionless golden ripples the National Hero passed, erect, solemn and gigantic, standing with folded arms in the stern of a slowly moving golden boat.

A long "Oh-h-h" burst from the spectators: the stand creaked and shook with their blissful trepidations. "Oh-h-h," Charity gasped: she had forgotten where she was, had at last forgotten even Harney's nearness. She seemed to have been caught up into the stars. . . .

The picture vanished and darkness came down. In the obscurity she felt her head clasped by two hands: her face was drawn backward, and Harney's lips were pressed on hers. With sudden vehemence he wound his arms about her, holding her head against his breast while she gave him back his kisses. An unknown Harney had revealed himself, a Harney who dominated her and yet over whom she felt herself possessed of a new mysterious power.

But the crowd was beginning to move, and he had to release her. "Come," he said in a confused voice. He scrambled over the side of the stand, and holding up his arm caught her as she sprang to the ground. He passed his arm about her waist, steadying her against the descending rush of people; and she clung to him, speechless, exultant, as if all the crowding and confusion about them were a mere vain stirring of the air.

"Come," he repeated, "we must try to make the trolley." He drew her along, and she followed, still in her dream. They walked as if they were one, so isolated in ecstasy that the people jostling them on every side seemed impalpable. But when they reached the terminus the illuminated trolley was already clanging on its way, its platforms black with passengers. The cars waiting behind it were as thickly packed;

and the throng about the terminus was so dense that it seemed hopeless to struggle for a place.

"Last trip up the Lake," a megaphone bellowed from the wharf; and the lights of the little steamboat came dancing out of the darkness.

"No use waiting here; shall we run up the Lake?" Harney suggested.

They pushed their way back to the edge of the water just as the gang-plank lowered from the white side of the boat. The electric light at the end of the wharf flashed full on the descending passengers, and among them Charity caught sight of Julia Hawes, her white feather askew, and the face under it flushed with coarse laughter. As she stepped from the gang-plank she stopped short, her dark-ringed eyes darting malice.

"Hullo, Charity Royall!" she called out; and then, looking back over her shoulder: "Didn't I tell you it was a family party? Here's grandpa's little daughter come to take him home!"

A snigger ran through the group; and then, towering above them, and steadying himself by the hand-rail in a desperate effort at erectness, Mr. Royall stepped stiffly ashore. Like the young men of the party, he wore a secret society emblem in the buttonhole of his black frockcoat.

His head was covered by a new Panama hat, and his narrow black tie, half undone, dangled down on his rumpled shirt-front. His face, a livid brown, with red blotches of anger and lips sunken in like an old man's, was a lamentable ruin in the searching glare.

He was just behind Julia Hawes, and had one hand on her arm; but as he left the gang-plank he freed himself, and moved a step or two away from his companions. He had seen Charity at once, and his glance passed slowly from her to Harney, whose arm was still about her. He stood staring at them, and trying to master the senile quiver of his lips; then he drew himself up with the tremulous majesty of drunkenness, and stretched out his arm.

"You whore — you damn — bare-headed whore, you!" he enunciated slowly.

There was a scream of tipsy laughter from the party, and Charity involuntarily put her hands to her head. She remembered that her hat had fallen from her lap when she jumped up to leave the stand; and suddenly she had a vision of herself, hatless, dishevelled, with a man's arm about her, confronting that drunken crew, headed by her guardian's pitiable figure. The picture filled her with shame. She had known since childhood about Mr. Royall's "habits": had seen him, as she went up to bed, sitting morosely in his office, a bottle at his elbow; or coming home, heavy and quarrelsome, from his business expeditions to Hepburn or Springfield; but the idea of his associating himself publicly with a band of disreputable girls and bar-room loafers was new and dreadful to her.

"Oh —" she said in a gasp of misery; and releasing herself from Harney's arm she went straight up to Mr. Royall.

"You come home with me — you come right home with me," she said in a low stern voice, as if she had not heard his apostrophe; and one of the girls called out: "Say, how many fellers does she want?"

There was another laugh, followed by a pause of curiosity, during which Mr. Royall continued to glare at Charity. At length his twitching lips parted. "I said, 'You — damn — whore!' " he repeated with precision, steadying himself on Julia's shoulder.

Laughs and jeers were beginning to spring up from the circle of people beyond their group; and a voice called out from the gangway: "Now, then, step lively there — all *aboard!*" The pressure of approaching and departing passengers forced the actors in the rapid scene apart, and pushed them back into the throng. Charity found herself clinging to Harney's arm and sobbing desperately. Mr. Royall had disappeared, and in the distance she heard the receding sound of Julia's laugh.

The boat, laden to the taffrail, was puffing away on her last trip.

XI

At two o'clock in the morning the freckled boy from Creston stopped his sleepy horse at the door of the red house, and Charity got out. Harney had taken leave of her at Creston River, charging the boy to drive her home. Her mind was still in a fog of misery, and she did not remember very clearly what had happened, or what they said to each other, during the interminable interval since their departure from Nettleton; but the secretive instinct of the animal in pain was so strong in her that she had a sense of relief when Harney got out and she drove on alone.

The full moon hung over North Dormer, whitening the mist that filled the hollows between the hills and floated transparently above the fields. Charity stood a moment at the gate, looking out into the waning night. She watched the boy drive off, his horse's head wagging heavily to and fro; then she went around to the kitchen door and felt under the mat for the key. She found it, unlocked the door and went in. The kitchen was dark, but she discovered a box of matches, lit a candle and went upstairs. Mr. Royall's door, opposite hers, stood open on his unlit room; evidently he had not come back. She went into her room, bolted her door and began slowly to untie the ribbon about her waist, and to take off her dress. Under the bed she saw the paper bag in which she had hidden her new hat from inquisitive eyes. . . .

She lay for a long time sleepless on her bed, staring up at the moonlight on the low ceiling; dawn was in the sky when she fell asleep, and when she woke the sun was on her face.

She dressed and went down to the kitchen. Verena was there alone: she glanced at Charity tranquilly, with her old deaf-looking eyes. There was no sign of Mr. Royall about the house and the hours passed without his reappearing. Charity had gone up to her room, and sat there listlessly, her hands on her lap. Puffs of sultry air fanned her dimity window curtains and flies buzzed stiflingly against the bluish panes.

At one o'clock Verena hobbled up to see if she were not coming down to dinner; but she shook her head, and the old woman went away, saying: "I'll cover up, then."

The sun turned and left her room, and Charity seated herself in the window, gazing down the village street through the half-opened shutters. Not a thought was in her mind; it was just a dark whirlpool of crowding images; and she watched the people passing along the street, Dan Targatt's team hauling a load of pine-trunks down to Hepburn, the sexton's old white horse grazing on the bank across the way, as if she looked at these familiar sights from the other side of the grave.

She was roused from her apathy by seeing Ally Hawes come out of the Frys' gate and walk slowly toward the red house with her uneven limping step. At the sight Charity recovered her severed contact with reality. She divined that Ally was coming to hear about her day: no one else was in the secret of the trip to Nettleton, and it had flattered Ally profoundly to be allowed to know of it.

At the thought of having to see her, of having to meet her eyes and answer or evade her questions, the whole horror of the previous night's adventure rushed back upon Charity. What had been a feverish nightmare became a cold and unescapable fact. Poor Ally, at that moment, represented North Dormer, with all its mean curiosities, its furtive malice, its sham unconsciousness of evil. Charity knew that, although all relations with Julia were supposed to be severed, the tender-hearted Ally still secretly communicated with her; and no doubt Julia would exult in the chance of retailing the scandal of the wharf. The story, exaggerated and distorted, was probably already on its way to North Dormer.

Ally's dragging pace had not carried her far from the Frys' gate when she was stopped by old Mrs. Sollas, who was a great talker, and spoke very slowly because she had never been able to get used to her new teeth from Hepburn. Still, even this respite would not last long; in another ten minutes Ally would be at the door, and Charity would hear her greeting Verena in the kitchen, and then calling up from the foot of the stairs.

Suddenly it became clear that flight, and instant flight, was the only thing conceivable. The longing to escape, to get away from familiar faces, from places where she was known, had always been strong in her in moments of distress. She had a childish belief in the miraculous power of strange scenes and new faces to transform her life and wipe out bitter memories. But such impulses were mere fleeting whims compared to the cold resolve which now possessed her. She felt she could not remain an hour longer under the roof of the man who had publicly dishonoured her, and face to face with the people who would presently be gloating over all the details of her humiliation.

Her passing pity for Mr. Royall had been swallowed up in loathing: everything in her recoiled from the disgraceful spectacle of the drunken old man apostrophizing her in the presence of a band of loafers and street-walkers. Suddenly, vividly, she relived again the horrible moment when he had tried to force himself into her room, and what she had before supposed to be a mad aberration now appeared to her as a vulgar incident in a debauched and degraded life.

While these thoughts were hurrying through her she had dragged out her old canvas school-bag, and was thrusting into it a few articles of clothing and the little packet of letters she had received from Harney. From under her pincushion she took the library key, and laid it in full view; then she felt at the back of a drawer for the blue brooch that Harney had given her. She would not have dared to wear it openly at North Dormer, but now she fastened it on her bosom as if it were a talisman to protect her in her flight. These preparations had taken but a few minutes, and when they were finished Ally Hawes was still at the Frys' corner talking to old Mrs. Sollas. . . .

She had said to herself, as she always said in moments of revolt: "I'll go to the Mountain — I'll go back to my own folks." She had never really meant it before; but now, as she considered her case, no other course seemed open. She had never learned any trade that would have given her independence in a strange place, and she knew no one in the big towns of the valley, where she might have hoped to find employment. Miss Hatchard was still away; but even had she been at North Dormer she was the last person to whom Charity would have turned, since one of the motives urging her to flight was the wish not to see Lucius Harney. Travelling back from Nettleton, in the crowded brightly-lit train, all exchange of confidence between them had been impossible; but during their drive from Hepburn to Creston River she had gathered from Harney's snatches of consolatory talk — again hampered by the freckled boy's presence — that he intended to see her the next day. At the moment she had found a vague comfort in the assurance; but in the desolate lucidity of the hours that followed she had come to see the impossibility of meeting him again. Her dream of comradeship was over; and the scene on the wharf — vile and disgraceful as it had been — had after all shed the light of truth on her minute of madness. It was as if her guardian's words had stripped her bare in the face of the grinning crowd and proclaimed to the world the secret admonitions of her conscience.

She did not think these things out clearly;

she simply followed the blind propulsion of her wretchedness. She did not want, ever again, to see anyone she had known; above all, she did not want to see Harney. . . .

She climbed the hill-path behind the house and struck through the woods by a shortcut leading to the Creston road. A lead sky hung heavily over the fields, and in the forest the motionless air was stifling; but she pushed on, impatient to reach the road which was the shortest way to the Mountain.

To do so, she had to follow the Creston road for a mile or two, and go within half a mile of the village; and she walked quickly, fearing to meet Harney. But there was no sign of him, and she had almost reached the branch road when she saw the flanks of a large white tent projecting through the trees by the roadside. She supposed that it sheltered a travelling circus which had come there for the Fourth; but as she drew nearer she saw, over the folded-back flap, a large sign bearing the inscription, "Gospel Tent." The interior seemed to be empty; but a young man in a black alpaca coat, his lank hair parted over a round white face, stepped from under the flap and advanced toward her with a smile.

"Sister, your Saviour knows everything. Won't you come in and lay your guilt before

Him?" he asked insinuatingly, putting his hand on her arm.

Charity started back and flushed. For a moment she thought the evangelist must have heard a report of the scene at Nettleton; then she saw the absurdity of the supposition.

"I on'y wish't I had any to lay!" she retorted, with one of her fierce flashes of self-derision; and the young man murmured, aghast: "Oh, Sister, don't speak blasphemy. . . ."

But she had jerked her arm out of his hold, and was running up the branch road, trembling with the fear of meeting a familiar face. Presently she was out of sight of the village, and climbing into the heart of the forest. She could not hope to do the fifteen miles to the Mountain that afternoon; but she knew of a place half-way to Hamblin where she could sleep, and where no one would think of looking for her. It was a little deserted house on a slope in one of the lonely rifts of the hills. She had seen it once, years before, when she had gone on a nutting expedition to the grove of walnuts below it. The party had taken refuge in the house from a sudden mountain storm, and she remembered that Ben Sollas, who liked frightening girls, had told them that it was said to be haunted.

She was growing faint and tired, for she

had eaten nothing since morning, and was not used to walking so far. Her head felt light and she sat down for a moment by the roadside. As she sat there she heard the click of a bicycle-bell, and started up to plunge back into the forest; but before she could move the bicycle had swept around the curve of the road, and Harney, jumping off, was approaching her with outstretched arms.

"Charity! What on earth are you doing here?"

She stared as if he were a vision, so startled by the unexpectedness of his being there that no words came to her.

"Where were you going? Had you forgotten that I was coming?" he continued, trying to draw her to him; but she shrank from his embrace.

"I was going away — I don't want to see you — I want you should leave me alone," she broke out wildly.

He looked at her and his face grew grave, as though the shadow of a premonition brushed it.

"Going away — from me, Charity?"

"From everybody. I want you should leave me."

He stood glancing doubtfully up and down the lonely forest road that stretched away into sun-flecked distances.

"Where were you going?"

"Home."

"Home — this way?"

She threw her head back defiantly. "To my home — up yonder: to the Mountain."

As she spoke she became aware of a change in his face. He was no longer listening to her, he was only looking at her, with the passionate absorbed expression she had seen in his eyes after they had kissed on the stand at Nettleton. He was the new Harney again, the Harney abruptly revealed in that embrace, who seemed so penetrated with the joy of her presence that he was utterly careless of what she was thinking or feeling.

He caught her hands with a laugh. "How do you suppose I found you?" he said gaily. He drew out the little packet of his letters and flourished them before her bewildered eyes.

"You dropped them, you imprudent young person — dropped them in the middle of the road, not far from here; and the young man who is running the Gospel tent picked them up just as I was riding by." He drew back, holding her at arm's length, and scrutinizing her troubled face with the minute searching gaze of his short-sighted eyes.

"Did you really think you could run away from me? You see you weren't meant to," he said; and before she could answer he had kissed her again, not vehemently, but tenderly, almost fraternally, as if he had guessed her confused pain, and wanted her to know he understood it. He wound his fingers through hers.

"Come — let's walk a little. I want to talk to you. There's so much to say."

He spoke with a boy's gaiety, carelessly and confidently, as if nothing had happened that could shame or embarrass them; and for a moment, in the sudden relief of her release from lonely pain, she felt herself yielding to his mood. But he had turned, and was drawing her back along the road by which she had come. She stiffened herself and stopped short.

"I won't go back," she said.

They looked at each other a moment in silence; then he answered gently: "Very well: let's go the other way, then."

She remained motionless, gazing silently at the ground, and he went on: "Isn't there a house up here somewhere — a little abandoned house — you meant to show me some day?" Still she made no answer, and he continued, in the same tone of tender reassurance: "Let us go there now and sit down and talk quietly." He took one of the hands that hung by her side and pressed his lips to the palm. "Do you suppose I'm going to let you send me away? Do you suppose I don't understand?"

The little old house — its wooden walls

sun-bleached to a ghostly grey — stood in an orchard above the road. The garden palings had fallen, but the broken gate dangled between its posts, and the path to the house was marked by rose-bushes run wild and hanging their small pale blossoms above the crowding grasses. Slender pilasters and an intricate fan-light framed the opening where the door had hung; and the door itself lay rotting in the grass, with an old apple-tree fallen across it.

Inside, also, wind and weather had blanched everything to the same wan silvery tint; the house was as dry and pure as the interior of a long-empty shell. But it must have been exceptionally well built, for the little rooms had kept something of their human aspect: the wooden mantels with their neat classic ornaments were in place, and the corners of one ceiling retained a light film of plaster tracery.

Harney had found an old bench at the back door and dragged it into the house. Charity sat on it, leaning her head against the wall in a state of drowsy lassitude. He had guessed that she was hungry and thirsty, and had brought her some tablets of chocolate from his bicycle-bag, and filled his drinking-cup from a spring in the orchard; and now he sat at her feet, smoking a cigarette, and looking up at her without speaking. Outside, the afternoon shadows were lengthening across the grass, and through the empty window-frame that faced her she saw the Mountain thrusting its dark mass against a sultry sunset. It was time to go.

She stood up, and he sprang to his feet also, and passed his arm through hers with an air of authority. "Now, Charity, you're coming back with me."

She looked at him and shook her head. "I ain't ever going back. You don't know."

"What don't I know?" She was silent, and he continued: "What happened on the wharf was horrible — it's natural you should feel as you do. But it doesn't make any real difference: you can't be hurt by such things. You must try to forget. And you must try to understand that men . . . men sometimes . . ."

"I know about men. That's why."

He coloured a little at the retort, as though it had touched him in a way she did not suspect.

"Well, then . . . you must know one has to make allowances. . . . He'd been drinking. . . ."

"I know all that, too. I've seen him so before. But he wouldn't have dared speak to me that way if he hadn't . . ."

"Hadn't what? What do you mean?"

"Hadn't wanted me to be like those other girls. . . ." She lowered her voice and looked away from him. "So's 't he wouldn't have to go out. . . ."

Harney stared at her. For a moment he did not seem to seize her meaning; then his face grew dark. "The damned hound! The villainous low hound!" His wrath blazed up, crimsoning him to the temples. "I never dreamed — good God, it's too vile," he broke off, as if his thoughts recoiled from the discovery.

"I won't never go back there," she repeated doggedly.

"No —" he assented.

There was a long interval of silence, during which she imagined that he was searching her face for more light on what she had revealed to him; and a flush of shame swept over her.

"I know the way you must feel about me," she broke out, ". . . telling you such things. . . ."

But once more, as she spoke, she became aware that he was no longer listening. He came close and caught her to him as if he were snatching her from some imminent peril: his impetuous eyes were in hers, and she could feel the hard beat of his heart as he held her against it.

"Kiss me again — like last night," he said, pushing her hair back as if to draw her whole face up into his kiss.

XII

One afternoon toward the end of August a group of girls sat in a room at Miss Hatchard's in a gay confusion of flags, turkey-red, blue and white paper muslin, harvest sheaves and illuminated scrolls.

North Dormer was preparing for its Old Home Week. That form of sentimental de-centralization was still in its early stages, and, precedents being few, and the desire to set an example contagious, the matter had become a subject of prolonged and passionate discussion under Miss Hatchard's roof. The incentive to the celebration had come rather from those who had left North Dormer than from those who had been obliged to stay there, and there was some difficulty in rousing the village to the proper state of enthusiasm. But Miss Hatchard's pale prim drawing-room was the centre of constant comings and goings from Hepburn, Nettleton, Springfield and even more distant cities; and whenever a visitor arrived he was led across the hall, and treated to a glimpse of the group of girls deep in their pretty preparations.

"All the old names . . . all the old names. . . ." Miss Hatchard would be heard, tapping across the hall on her crutches. "Targatt . . . Sollas . . . Fry: this is Miss Orma Fry sewing the stars on the drapery for the organ-loft. Don't move, girls . . . and this is Miss Ally Hawes, our cleverest needle-woman . . . and Miss Charity Royall making our garlands of evergreen. . . . I like the idea of its all being home-made, don't you? We haven't had to call in any foreign talent: my young cousin Lucius Harney, the archi-tect — you know he's up here preparing a book on Colonial houses — he's taken the whole thing in hand so cleverly; but you must come and see his sketch for the stage we're going to put up in the Town Hall."

One of the first results of the Old Home Week agitation had, in fact, been the reap-pearance of Lucius Harney in the village street. He had been vaguely spoken of as being not far off, but for some weeks past no one had seen him at North Dormer, and there was a recent report of his having left Creston River, where he was said to have been staying, and gone away from the neighbourhood for good. Soon after Miss Hatchard's return, however, he came back to his old quarters in her house, and began to take a leading part in the planning of the festivities. He threw himself into the idea with extraordinary good-humour, and was so prodigal of sketches, and so inexhaustible in devices, that he gave an immediate impetus to the rather languid movement, and infected the whole village with his enthusiasm.

"Lucius has such a feeling for the past that he has roused us all to a sense of our privileges," Miss Hatchard would say, lingering on the last word, which was a favourite one. And before leading her visitor back to the drawing-room she would repeat, for the hundredth time, that she supposed he thought it very bold of little North Dormer to start up and have a Home Week of its own, when so many bigger places hadn't thought of it yet; but that, after all, Associations counted more than the size of the population, didn't they? And of course North Dormer was so full of Associations . . . historic, literary (here a filial sigh for Honorius) and ecclesiastical . . . he knew about the old pewter communion service imported from England in 1769, she supposed? And it was so important, in a wealthy materialistic age, to set the example of reverting to the old ideals, the family and the homestead, and so on. This peroration usually carried her half-way back across the hall, leaving the girls to return to their interrupted activities.

The day on which Charity Royall was weaving hemlock garlands for the proces-

156

sion was the last before the celebration. When Miss Hatchard called upon the North Dormer maidenhood to collaborate in the festal preparations Charity had at first held aloof; but it had been made clear to her that her non-appearance might excite conjecture, and, reluctantly, she had joined the other workers. The girls, at first shy and embarrassed, and puzzled as to the exact nature of the projected commemoration, had soon become interested in the amusing details of their task, and excited by the notice they received. They would not for the world have missed their afternoons at Miss Hatchard's, and, while they cut out and sewed and draped and pasted, their tongues kept up such an accompaniment to the sewing-machine that Charity's silence sheltered itself unperceived under their chatter.

In spirit she was still almost unconscious of the pleasant stir about her. Since her return to the red house, on the evening of the day when Harney had overtaken her on her way to the Mountain, she had lived at North Dormer as if she were suspended in the void. She had come back there because Harney, after appearing to agree to the impossibility of her doing so, had ended by persuading her that any other course would be madness. She had nothing further to fear from Mr. Royall. Of this she had declared herself sure, though she had failed to add, in his exoneration, that he had twice offered to make her his wife. Her hatred of him made it impossible, at the moment, for her to say anything that might partly excuse him in Harney's eyes.

Harney, however, once satisfied of her security, had found plenty of reasons for urging her to return. The first, and the most unanswerable, was that she had nowhere else to go. But the one on which he laid the greatest stress was that flight would be equivalent to avowal. If — as was almost inevitable — rumours of the scandalous scene at Nettleton should reach North Dormer, how else would her disappearance be interpreted? Her guardian had publicly taken away her character, and she immediately vanished from his house. Seekers after motives could hardly fail to draw an unkind conclusion. But if she came back at once, and was seen leading her usual life, the incident was reduced to its true proportions, as the outbreak of a drunken old man furious at being surprised in disreputable company. People would say that Mr. Royall had insulted his ward to justify himself, and the sordid tale would fall into its place in the chronicle of his obscure debaucheries.

Charity saw the force of the argument; but if she acquiesced it was not so much because of that as because it was Harney's wish. Since that evening in the deserted house she could imagine no reason for doing or not doing anything except the fact that Harney wished or did not wish it. All her tossing contradictory impulses were merged in a fatalistic acceptance of his will. It was not that she felt in him any ascendency of character — there were moments already when she knew she was the stronger — but that all the rest of life had become a mere cloudy rim about the central glory of their passion. Whenever she stopped thinking about that for a moment she felt as she sometimes did after lying on the grass and staring up too long at the sky; her eyes were so full of light that everything about her was a blur.

Each time that Miss Hatchard, in the course of her periodical incursions into the work-room, dropped an allusion to her young cousin, the architect, the effect was the same on Charity. The hemlock garland she was wearing fell to her knees and she sat in a kind of trance. It was so manifestly absurd that Miss Hatchard should talk of Harney in that familiar possessive way, as if she had any claim on him, or knew anything about him. She, Charity Royall, was the only being on earth who really knew him, knew him from the soles of his feet to the rumpled crest of his hair, knew the shifting lights in his eyes, and the inflections of his voice, and the things he liked and disliked, and everything there was to know about him, as minutely and yet unconsciously as a child knows the walls of the room it wakes up in every morning. It was this fact, which nobody about her guessed, or would have understood, that made her life something apart and inviolable, as if nothing had any power to hurt or disturb her as long as her secret was safe.

The room in which the girls sat was the one which had been Harney's bedroom. He had been sent upstairs, to make room for the Home Week workers; but the furniture had not been moved, and as Charity sat there she had perpetually before her the vision she had looked in on from the midnight garden. The table at which Harney had sat was the one about which the girls were gathered; and her own seat was near the bed on which she had seen him lying. Sometimes, when the others were not looking, she bent over as if to pick up something, and laid her cheek for a moment against the pillow.

Toward sunset the girls disbanded. Their work was done, and the next morning at daylight the draperies and garlands were to be nailed up, and the illuminated scrolls put in place in the Town Hall. The first

160

guests were to drive over from Hepburn in time for the midday banquet under a tent in Miss Hatchard's field; and after that the ceremonies were to begin. Miss Hatchard, pale with fatigue and excitement, thanked her young assistants, and stood on the porch, leaning on her crutches and waving a farewell as she watched them troop away down the street.

Charity had slipped off among the first; but at the gate she heard Ally Hawes calling after her, and reluctantly turned.

"Will you come over now and try on your dress?" Ally asked, looking at her with wistful admiration. "I want to be sure the sleeves don't ruck up the same as they did yesterday."

Charity gazed at her with dazzled eyes. "Oh, it's lovely," she said, and hastened away without listening to Ally's protest. She wanted her dress to be as pretty as the other girls' — wanted it, in fact, to outshine the rest, since she was to take part in the "exercises" — but she had no time just then to fix her mind on such matters. . . .

She sped up the street to the library, of which she had the key about her neck. From the passage at the back she dragged forth a bicycle, and guided it to the edge of the street. She looked about to see if any of the girls were approaching; but they had drifted away together toward the Town Hall, and she sprang into the saddle and turned toward the Creston road. There was an almost continual descent to Creston, and with her feet against the pedals she floated through the still evening air like one of the hawks she had often watched slanting downward on motionless wings. Twenty minutes from the time when she had left Miss Hatchard's door she was turning up the wood-road on which Harney had over-taken her on the day of her flight; and a few minutes afterward she had jumped from her bicycle at the gate of the deserted house.

In the gold-powdered sunset it looked more than ever like some frail shell dried and washed by many seasons; but at the back, whither Charity advanced, drawing her bicycle after her, there were signs of recent habitation. A rough door made of boards hung in the kitchen doorway, and pushing it open she entered a room fur-nished in primitive camping fashion. In the window was a table, also made of boards, with an earthenware jar holding a big bunch of wild asters, two canvas chairs stood near by, and in one corner was a mattress with a Mexican blanket over it.

The room was empty, and leaning her bicycle against the house Charity clam-bered up the slope and sat down on a rock under an old apple-tree. The air was perfectly still, and from where she sat she would be able to hear the tinkle of a bicycle-bell a long way down the road. . . .

She was always glad when she got to the little house before Harney. She liked to have time to take in every detail of its secret sweetness — the shadows of the apple-trees swaying on the grass, the old walnuts rounding their domes below the road, the meadows sloping westward in the afternoon light — before his first kiss blotted it all out. Everything unrelated to the hours spent in that tranquil place was as faint as the remembrance of a dream. The only reality was the wondrous unfolding of her new self, the reaching out to the light of all her contracted tendrils. She had lived all her life among people whose sensibilities seemed to have withered for lack of use; and more wonderful, at first, than Harney's endearments were the words that were a part of them. She had always thought of love as something confused and furtive, and he made it as bright and open as the summer air.

On the morrow of the day when she had shown him the way to the deserted house he had packed up and left Creston River for Boston; but at the first station he had jumped off the train with a hand-bag and scrambled up into the hills. For two golden rainless August weeks he had camped in the house, getting eggs and milk from the solitary farm in the valley, where no one knew him, and doing his cooking over a spirit-lamp. He got up every day with the sun, took a plunge in a brown pool he knew of, and spent long hours lying in the scented hemlock-woods above the house, or wandering along the yoke of the Eagle Ridge, far above the misty blue valleys that swept away east and west between the endless hills. And in the afternoon Charity came to him.

With part of what was left of her savings she had hired a bicycle for a month, and every day after dinner, as soon as her guardian started to his office, she hurried to the library, got out her bicycle, and flew down the Creston road. She knew that Mr. Royall, like everyone else in North Dormer, was perfectly aware of her acquisition: possibly he, as well as the rest of the village, knew what use she made of it. She did not care: she felt him to be so powerless that if he had questioned her she would probably have told him the truth. But they had never spoken to each other since the night on the wharf at Nettleton. He had returned to North Dormer only on the third day after that encounter, arriving just as Charity and Verena were sitting down to supper. He had drawn up his chair, taken his napkin from the sideboard drawer, pulled it out of its ring, and seated himself as unconcernedly as if he had come in from his usual afternoon session at Carrick Fry's; and the long habit of the household made it seem almost natural that Charity should not so much as raise her eyes when he entered. She had simply let him understand that her silence was not accidental by leaving the table while he was still eating, and going up without a word to shut herself into her room. After that he formed the habit of talking loudly and genially to Verena whenever Charity was in the room; but otherwise there was no apparent change in their relations.

She did not think connectedly of these things while she sat waiting for Harney, but they remained in her mind as a sullen background against which her short hours with him flamed out like forest fires. Nothing else mattered, neither the good nor the bad, or what might have seemed so before she knew him. He had caught her up and carried her away into a new world, from which, at stated hours, the ghost of her came back to perform certain customary acts, but all so thinly and insubstantially that she sometimes wondered that the people she went about among could see her. . . .

Behind the swarthy Mountain the sun had gone down in waveless gold. From a pasture up the slope a tinkle of cow-bells sounded; a puff of smoke hung over the farm in the valley, trailed on the pure air and was gone. For a few minutes, in the clear light that is all shadow, fields and woods were outlined with an unreal precision; then the twilight blotted them out, and the little house turned grey and spectral under its wizened apple-branches.

Charity's heart contracted. The first fall of night after a day of radiance often gave her a sense of hidden menace: it was like looking out over the world as it would be when love had gone from it. She wondered if some day she would sit in that same place and watch in vain for her lover. . . .

His bicycle-bell sounded down the lane, and in a minute she was at the gate and his eyes were laughing in hers. They walked back through the long grass, and pushed open the door behind the house. The room at first seemed quite dark and they had to grope their way in hand in hand. Through the window-frame the sky looked light by contrast, and above the black mass of asters in the earthern jar one white star glimmered like a moth.

"There was such a lot to do at the last minute," Harney was explaining, "and I had to drive down to Creston to meet someone who has come to stay with my cousin for the show."

166

He had his arms about her, and his kisses were in her hair and on her lips. Under his touch things deep down in her struggled to the light and sprang up like flowers in sunshine. She twisted her fingers into his, and they sat down side by side on the improvised couch. She hardly heard his excuses for being late: in his absence a thousand doubts tormented her, but as soon as he appeared she ceased to wonder where he had come from, what had delayed him, who had kept him from her. It seemed as if the places he had been in, and the people he had been with, must cease to exist when he left them, just as her own life was suspended in his absence.

He continued, now, to talk to her volubly and gaily, deploring his lateness, grumbling at the demands on his time, and good-humouredly mimicking Miss Hatchard's benevolent agitation. "She hurried off Miles to ask Mr. Royall to speak at the Town Hall tomorrow: I didn't know till it was done." Charity was silent, and he added: "After all, perhaps it's just as well. No one else could have done it."

Charity made no answer: She did not care what part her guardian played in the morrow's ceremonies. Like all the other figures peopling her meagre world he had grown non-existent to her. She had even put off hating him.

"Tomorrow I shall only see you from far off," Harney continued. "But in the evening there'll be the dance in the Town Hall. Do you want me to promise not to dance with any other girl?"

Any other girl? Were there any others? She had forgotten even that peril, so enclosed did he and she seem in their secret world. Her heart gave a frightened jerk.

"Yes, promise."

He laughed and took her in his arms. "You goose — not even if they're hideous?"

He pushed the hair from her forehead, bending her face back, as his way was, and leaning over so that his head loomed black between her eyes and the paleness of the sky, in which the white star floated . . .

Side by side they sped back along the dark wood-road to the village. A late moon was rising, full orbed and fiery, turning the mountain ranges from fluid grey to a massive blackness, and making the upper sky so light that the stars looked as faint as their own reflections in water. At the edge of the wood, half a mile from North Dormer, Harney jumped from his bicycle, took Charity in his arms for a last kiss, and then waited while she went on alone.

They were later than usual, and instead of taking the bicycle to the library she propped it against the back of the wood-shed and entered the kitchen of the red house. Verena sat there alone; when Charity came in she looked at her with mild impenetrable eyes and then took a plate and a glass of milk from the shelf and set them silently on the table. Charity nodded her thanks, and sitting down, fell hungrily upon her piece of pie and emptied the glass. Her face burned with her quick flight through the night, and her eyes were dazzled by the twinkle of the kitchen lamp. She felt like a night-bird suddenly caught and caged.

"He ain't come back since supper," Verena said. "He's down to the Hall."

Charity took no notice. Her soul was still winging through the forest. She washed her plate and tumbler, and then felt her way up the dark stairs. When she opened her door a wonder arrested her. Before going out she had closed her shutters against the afternoon heat, but they had swung partly open, and a bar of moonlight, crossing the room, rested on her bed and showed a dress of China silk laid out on it in virgin whiteness. Charity had spent more than she could afford on the dress, which was to surpass those of all the other girls; she had wanted to let North Dormer see that she was worthy of Harney's admiration. Above the dress, folded on the pillow, was the white veil which the young women who took part in the exercises were to wear under a wreath of asters; and beside the veil a pair of slim white satin shoes that Ally had produced from an old trunk in which she stored mysterious treasures.

Charity stood gazing at all the outspread whiteness. It recalled a vision that had come to her in the night after her first meeting with Harney. She no longer had such visions . . . warmer splendours had displaced them . . . but it was stupid of Ally to have paraded all those white things on her bed, exactly as Hattie Targatt's wedding dress from Springfield had been spread out for the neighbours to see when she married Tom Fry. . . .

Charity took up the satin shoes and looked at them curiously. By day, no doubt, they would appear a little worn, but in the moonlight they seemed carved of ivory. She sat down on the floor to try them on, and they fitted her perfectly, though when she stood up she lurched a little on the high heels. She looked down at her feet, which the graceful mould of the slippers had marvellously arched and narrowed. She had never seen such shoes before, even in the shop-windows at Nettleton . . . never, except . . . yes, once, she had noticed a pair of the same shape on Annabel Balch.

A blush of mortification swept over her. Ally sometimes sewed for Miss Balch when that brilliant being descended on North Dormer, and no doubt she picked up presents of cast-off clothing: the treasures in the mysterious trunk all came from the people she worked for; there could be no doubt that the white slippers were Annabel Balch's. . . .

As she stood there, staring down moodily at her feet, she heard the triple click-click-click of a bicycle-bell under her window. It was Harney's secret signal as he passed on his way home. She stumbled to the window on her high heels, flung open the shutters and leaned out. He waved to her and sped by, his black shadow dancing merrily ahead of him down the empty moonlit road; and she leaned there watching him till he vanished under the Hatchard spruces.

XIII

The Town Hall was crowded and exceedingly hot. As Charity marched into it third in the white muslin file headed by Orma Fry, she was conscious mainly of the brilliant effect of the wreathed columns framing the green-carpeted stage toward which she was moving; and of the unfamiliar faces turning from the front rows to watch the advance of the procession.

But it was all a bewildering blur of eyes and colours till she found herself standing at the back of the stage, her great bunch of asters and goldenrod held well in front of her, and answering the nervous glance of Lambert Sollas, the organist from Mr. Miles's church, who had come up from Nettleton to play the harmonium and sat behind it, his conductor's eye running over the fluttered girls.

A moment later Mr. Miles, pink and twinkling, emerged from the background, as if buoyed up on his broad white gown, and briskly dominated the bowed heads in the front rows. He prayed energetically and briefly and then retired, and a fierce nod from Lambert Sollas warned the girls that they were to follow at once with "Home, Sweet Home." It was a joy to Charity to sing: it seemed as though, for the first time, her secret rapture might burst from her and flash its defiance at the world. All the glow in her blood, the breath of the summer earth, the rustle of the forest, the fresh call of birds at sunrise, and the brooding midday languors, seemed to pass into her untrained voice, lifted and led by the sustaining chorus.

And then suddenly the song was over, and after an uncertain pause, during which Miss Hatchard's pearl-grey gloves started a furtive signalling down the hall, Mr. Royall, emerging in turn, ascended the steps of the stage and appeared behind the flower-wreathed desk. He passed close to Charity, and she noticed that his gravely set face wore the look of majesty that used to awe and fascinate her childhood. His frock-coat had been carefully brushed and ironed, and the ends of his narrow black tie were so nearly even that the tying must have cost him a protracted struggle. His appearance struck her all the more because it was the first time she had looked him full in the face since the night at Nettleton, and nothing in his grave and impressive demeanour revealed a trace of the lamentable figure on the wharf.

He stood a moment behind the desk, resting his fingertips against it, and bending slightly toward his audience; then he straightened himself and began.

At first she paid no heed to what he was saying: only fragments of sentences, sonorous quotations, allusions to illustrious men, including the obligatory tribute to Honorius Hatchard, drifted past her inattentive ears. She was trying to discover Harney among the notable people in the front row; but he was nowhere near Miss Hatchard, who, crowned by a pearl-grey hat that matched her gloves, sat just below the desk, supported by Mrs. Miles and an important-looking unknown lady. Charity was near one end of the stage, and from where she sat the other end of the first row of seats was cut off by the screen of foliage masking the harmonium. The effort to see Harney around the corner of the screen, or through its interstices, made her unconscious of everything else; but the effort was unsuccessful, and gradually she found her attention arrested by her guardian's discourse.

She had never heard him speak in public before, but she was familiar with the rolling music of his voice when he read aloud, or held forth to the selectmen about the stove at Carrick Fry's. Today his inflections were richer and graver than she had ever known them: he spoke slowly, with pauses that seemed to invite his hearers to silent participation in his thought; and Charity perceived a light of response in their faces.

He was nearing the end of his address . . . "Most of you," he said, "most of you who have returned here today, to take contact with this little place for a brief hour, have come only on a pious pilgrimage, and will go back presently to busy cities and lives full of larger duties. But that is not the only way of coming back to North Dormer. Some of us, who went out from here in our youth . . . went out, like you, to busy cities and larger duties . . . have come back in another way — come back for good. I am one of those, as many of you know. . . ." He paused, and there was a sense of suspense in the listening hall. "My history is without interest, but it has its lesson: not so much for those of you who have already made your lives in other places, as for the young men who are perhaps planning even now to leave these quiet hills and go down into the struggle. Things they cannot foresee may send some of those young men back some day to the little township and the old homestead: they may come back for good. . . ." He looked about him, and repeated gravely: "For *good.* There's the point I want to make . . . North Dormer is a poor little place, almost lost in a mighty landscape:

perhaps, by this time, it might have been a bigger place, and more in scale with the landscape, if those who had to come back had come with that feeling in their minds — that they wanted to come back for *good* . . . and not for bad . . . or just for indifference. . . .

"Gentlemen, let us look at things as they are. Some of us have come back to our native town because we'd failed to get on elsewhere. One way or other, things had gone wrong with us . . . what we'd dreamed of hadn't come true. But the fact that we had failed elsewhere is no reason why we should fail here. Our very experiments in larger places, even if they were unsuccessful, ought to have helped us to make North Dormer a larger place . . . and you young men who are preparing even now to follow the call of ambition, and turn your back on the old homes — well, let me say this to you, that if ever you do come back to them it's worth while to come back to them for their good. . . . And to do that, you must keep on loving them while you're away from them; and even if you come back against your will — and thinking it's all a bitter mistake of Fate or Providence — you must try to make the best of it, and to make the best of your old town; and after a while — well, ladies and gentlemen, I give you my recipe for what it's worth; after a while, I believe you'll be able to say, as I can say today: 'I'm glad I'm here.' Believe me, all of you, the best way to help the places we live in is to be glad we live there."

He stopped, and a murmur of emotion and surprise ran through the audience. It was not in the least what they had expected, but it moved them more than what they had expected would have moved them. "Hear, hear!" a voice cried out in the middle of the hall. An outburst of cheers caught up the cry, and as they subsided Charity heard Mr. Miles saying to someone near him: "That was a *man* talking —" He wiped his spectacles.

Mr. Royall had stepped back from the desk, and taken his seat in the row of chairs in front of the harmonium. A dapper white-haired gentleman — a distant Hatchard — succeeded him behind the goldenrod, and began to say beautiful things about the old oaken bucket, patient white-haired mothers, and where the boys used to go nutting . . . and Charity began again to search for Harney. . . .

Suddenly Mr. Royall pushed back his seat, and one of the maple branches in front of the harmonium collapsed with a crash. It uncovered the end of the first row and in one of the seats Charity saw Harney, and in the next a lady whose face was turned toward him, and almost hidden by the brim of her drooping hat. Charity did not need to see the face. She knew at a glance the slim figure, the fair hair heaped up under the hat-brim, the long pale wrinkled gloves with bracelets slipping over them. At the fall of the branch Miss Balch turned her head toward the stage, and in her pretty thin-lipped smile there lingered the reflection of something her neighbour had been whispering to her. . . .

Someone came forward to replace the fallen branch, and Miss Balch and Harney were once more hidden. But to Charity the vision of their two faces had blotted out everything. In a flash they had shown her the bare reality of her situation. Behind the frail screen of her lover's caresses was the whole inscrutable mystery of his life: his relations with other people — with other women — his opinions, his prejudices, his principles, the net of influences and interests and ambitions in which every man's life is entangled. Of all these she knew nothing, except what he had told her of his architectural aspirations. She had always dimly guessed him to be in touch with important people, involved in complicated relations — but she felt it all to be so far beyond her understanding that the whole subject hung like a luminous mist on the farthest verge of her thought. In the foreground, hiding all else, there was the glow of his presence, the light and shadow of his face, the way his short-sighted eyes, at her approach, widened and deepened as if to draw her down into them; and, above all, the flush of youth and tenderness in which his words enclosed her.

Now she saw him detached from her, drawn back into the unknown, and whispering to another girl things that provoked the same smile of mischievous complicity he had so often called to her own lips. The feeling possessing her was not one of jealousy: she was too sure of his love. It was rather a terror of the unknown, of all the mysterious attractions that must even now be dragging him away from her, and of her own powerlessness to contend with them.

She had given him all she had — but what was it compared to the other gifts life held for him? She understood now the case of girls like herself to whom this kind of thing happened. They gave all they had, but their all was not enough: it could not buy more than a few moments. . . .

The heat had grown suffocating — she felt it descend on her in smothering waves, and the faces in the crowded hall began to dance like the pictures flashed on the screen at Nettleton. For an instant Mr. Royall's countenance detached itself from the general blur. He had resumed his place in front of the harmonium, and sat close to her, his eyes on her face; and his look seemed to pierce to the very centre of her confused sensations. . . . A feeling of physical sickness rushed over her — and then deadly apprehension. The light of the fiery hours in the little house swept back on her in a glare of fear. . . .

She forced herself to look away from her guardian, and became aware that the oratory of the Hatchard cousin had ceased, and that Mr. Miles was again flapping his wings. Fragments of his peroration floated through her bewildered brain. . . . "A rich harvest of hallowed memories. . . . A sanctified hour to which, in moments of trial, your thoughts will prayerfully return. . . . And now, O Lord, let us humbly and fervently give thanks for this blessed day of reunion, here in the old home to which we have come back from so far. Preserve it to us, O Lord, in times to come, in all its homely sweetness — in the kindliness and wisdom of its old people, in the courage and industry of its young men, in the piety and purity of this group of innocent girls —" He flapped a white wing in their direction, and at the same moment Lambert Sollas, with his fierce nod, struck the opening bars of "Auld Lang Syne." . . . Charity stared straight ahead of her and then, dropping her flowers, fell face downward at Mr. Royall's feet.

XIV

North Dormer's celebration naturally included the villages attached to its township, and the festivities were to radiate over the whole group, from Dormer and the two Crestons to Hamblin, the lonely hamlet on the north slope of the Mountain where the first snow always fell. On the third day there were speeches and ceremonies at Creston and Creston River; on the fourth the principal performers were to be driven in buckboards to Dormer and Hamblin.

It was on the fourth day that Charity returned for the first time to the little house. She had not seen Harney alone since they had parted at the wood's edge the night before the celebrations began. In the interval she had passed through many moods, but for the moment the terror which had seized her in the Town Hall had faded to the edge of consciousness. She had fainted because the hall was stiflingly hot, and because the speakers had gone on and on. . . . Several other people had been affected by the heat, and had had to leave before the exercises were over. There had been thunder in the air all the afternoon, and everyone said afterward that something ought to have been done to ventilate the hall. . . .

At the dance that evening — where she had gone reluctantly, and only because she feared to stay away, she had sprung back into instant reassurance. As soon as she entered she had seen Harney waiting for her, and he had come up with kind gay eyes, and swept her off in a waltz. Her feet were full of music, and though her only training had been with the village youths she had no difficulty in tuning her steps to his. As they circled about the floor all her vain fears dropped from her, and she even forgot that she was probably dancing in Annabel Balch's slippers.

When the waltz was over Harney, with a last handclasp, left her to meet Miss Hatchard and Miss Balch, who were just entering. Charity had a moment of anguish as Miss Balch appeared; but it did not last. The triumphant fact of her own greater beauty, and of Harney's sense of it, swept her apprehensions aside. Miss Balch, in an unbecoming dress, looked sallow and pinched, and Charity fancied there was a worried expression in her pale-lashed eyes. She took a seat near Miss Hatchard and it was presently apparent that she did not mean to dance. Charity did not dance often either. Harney explained to her that Miss Hatchard had begged him to give each of the other girls a turn; but he went through the form of asking Charity's permission each time he led one out, and that gave her a sense of secret triumph even completer than when she was whirling about the room with him. . . .

She was thinking of all this as she waited for him in the deserted house. The late afternoon was sultry, and she had tossed aside her hat and stretched herself at full length on the Mexican blanket because it was cooler indoors than under the trees. She lay with her arms folded beneath her head, gazing out at the shaggy shoulder of the Mountain. The sky behind it was full of the splintered glories of the descending sun, and before long she expected to hear Harney's bicycle-bell in the lane. He had bicycled to Hamblin, instead of driving there with his cousin and her friends, so that he might be able to make his escape earlier and stop on the way back at the deserted house, which was on the road to Hamblin. They had smiled together at the joke of hearing the crowded buckboards roll by on the return, while they lay close in their hiding above the road. Such childish triumphs still gave her a sense of reckless security.

Nevertheless she had not wholly forgotten

the vision of fear that had opened before her in the Town Hall. The sense of lastingness was gone from her and every moment with Harney would now be ringed with doubt.

The Mountain was turning purple against a fiery sunset from which it seemed to be divided by a knife-edge of quivering light; and above this wall of flame the whole sky was a pure pale green, like some cold mountain lake in shadow. Charity lay gazing up at it, and watching for the first white star. . . .

Her eyes were still fixed on the upper reaches of the sky when she became aware that a shadow had flitted across the glory-flooded room: it must have been Harney passing the window against the sunset. . . . She half raised herself, and then dropped back on her folded arms. The combs had slipped from her hair, and it trailed in a rough dark rope across her breast. She lay quite still, a sleepy smile on her lips, her indolent lids half shut. There was a fumbling at the padlock and she called out: "Have you slipped the chain?" The door opened, and Mr. Royall walked into the room.

She started up, sitting back against the cushions, and they looked at each other without speaking. Then Mr. Royall closed the door-latch and advanced a few steps.

Charity jumped to her feet. "What have you come for?" she stammered.

The last glare of the sunset was on her guardian's face, which looked ash-coloured in the yellow radiance.

"Because I knew you were here," he answered simply.

She had become conscious of the hair hanging loose across her breast, and it seemed as though she could not speak to him till she had set herself in order. She groped for her comb, and tried to fasten up the coil. Mr. Royall silently watched her.

"Charity," he said, "he'll be here in a minute. Let me talk to you first."

"You've got no right to talk to me. I can do what I please."

"Yes. What is it you mean to do?"

"I needn't answer that, or anything else."

He had glanced away, and stood looking curiously about the illuminated room. Purple asters and red-maple-leaves filled the jar on the table; on a shelf against the wall stood a lamp, the kettle, a little pile of cups and saucers. The canvas chairs were grouped about the table.

"So this is where you meet," he said.

His tone was quiet and controlled, and the fact disconcerted her. She had been ready to give him violence for violence, but this calm acceptance of things as they were left her without a weapon.

"See here, Charity — you're always telling me I've got no rights over you. There might be two ways of looking at that — but I ain't going to argue it. All I know is I raised you as good as I could, and meant fairly by you always — except once, for a bad half-hour. There's no justice in weighing that half-hour against the rest, and you know it. If you hadn't, you wouldn't have gone on living under my roof. Seems to me the fact of your doing that gives me some sort of a right; the right to try and keep you out of trouble. I'm not asking you to consider any other."

She listened in silence, and then gave a slight laugh. "Better wait till I'm in trouble," she said.

He paused a moment, as if weighing her words. "Is that all your answer?"

"Yes, that's all."

"Well — I'll wait."

He turned away slowly, but as he did so the thing she had been waiting for happened; the door opened again and Harney entered.

He stopped short with a face of astonishment, and then, quickly controlling himself, went up to Mr. Royall with a frank look.

"Have you come to see me, sir?" he said coolly, throwing his cap on the table with an air of proprietorship.

Mr. Royall again looked slowly about the

room; then his eyes turned to the young man.

"Is this your house?" he inquired.

Harney laughed: "Well — as much as it's anybody's. I come here to sketch occasionally."

"And to receive Miss Royall's visits?"

"When she does me the honour —"

"Is this the home you propose to bring her to when you get married?"

There was an immense and oppressive silence. Charity, quivering with anger, started forward, and then stood silent, too humbled for speech. Harney's eyes had dropped under the old man's gaze; but he raised them presently, and looking steadily at Mr. Royall, said: "Miss Royall is not a child. Isn't it rather absurd to talk of her as if she were? I believe she considers herself free to come and go as she pleases, without any questions from anyone." He paused and added: "I'm ready to answer any she wishes to ask me."

Mr. Royall turned to her. "Ask him when he's going to marry you, then —" There was another silence, and he laughed in his turn — a broken laugh, with a scraping sound in it. "You darsn't!" he shouted out with sudden passion. He went close up to Charity, his right arm lifted, not in menace but in tragic exhortation.

"You darsn't, and you know it — and you

know why!" He swung back again upon the young man. "And you know why you ain't asked her to marry you, and why you don't mean to. It's because you hadn't need to; nor any other man either. I'm the only one that was fool enough not to know that; and I guess nobody'll repeat my mistake — not in Eagle County, anyhow. They all know what she is, and what she came from. They all know her mother was a woman of the town from Nettleton, that followed one of those Mountain fellows up to his place and lived there with him like a heathen. I saw her there sixteen years ago, when I went to bring this child down. I went to save her from the kind of life her mother was leading — but I'd better have left her in the kennel she came from. . . ." He paused and stared darkly at the two young people, and out beyond them, at the menacing Mountain with its rim of fire; then he sat down beside the table on which they had so often spread their rustic supper, and covered his face with his hands. Harney leaned in the window, a frown on his face: he was twirling between his fingers a small package that dangled from a loop of string. . . . Charity heard Mr. Royall draw a hard breath or two, and his shoulders shook a little. Presently he stood up and walked across the room. He did not look again at the young people: they saw him feel his way to the door and fumble for the latch; and then he went out into the darkness.

After he had gone there was a long silence. Charity waited for Harney to speak; but he seemed at first not to find anything to say. At length he broke out irrelevantly: "I wonder how he found out?"

She made no answer and he tossed down the package he had been holding, and went up to her.

"I'm so sorry, dear . . . that this should have happened. . . ."

She threw her head back proudly. "I ain't ever been sorry — not a minute!"

"No."

She waited to be caught into his arms, but he turned away from her irresolutely. The last glow was gone from behind the Mountain. Everything in the room had turned grey and indistinct, and an autumnal dampness crept up from the hollow below the orchard, laying its cold touch on their flushed faces. Harney walked the length of the room, and then turned back and sat down at the table.

"Come," he said imperiously.

She sat down beside him, and he untied the string about the package and spread out a pile of sandwiches.

"I stole them from the love-feast at Hamblin," he said with a laugh, pushing them over to her. She laughed too, and took one,

189

and began to eat.

"Didn't you make the tea?"

"No," she said. "I forgot —"

"Oh, well — it's too late to boil the water now." He said nothing more, and sitting opposite to each other they went on silently eating the sandwiches. Darkness had descended in the little room, and Harney's face was a dim blur to Charity. Suddenly he leaned across the table and laid his hand on hers.

"I shall have to go off for a while — a month or two, perhaps — to arrange some things; and then I'll come back . . . and we'll get married."

His voice seemed like a stranger's: nothing was left in it of the vibrations she knew. Her hand lay inertly under his, and she left it there, and raised her head, trying to answer him. But the words died in her throat. They sat motionless, in their attitude of confident endearment, as if some strange death had surprised them. At length Harney sprang to his feet with a slight shiver. "God! it's damp — we couldn't have come here much longer." He went to the shelf, took down a tin candle-stick and lit the candle; then he propped an unhinged shutter against the empty window-frame and put the candle on the table. It threw up a queer shadow on his frowning forehead, and made the smile on his lips a grimace.

"But it's been good, though, hasn't it, Charity? . . . What's the matter — why do you stand there staring at me? Haven't the days here been good?" He went up to her and caught her to his breast. "And there'll be others — lots of others . . . jollier . . . even jollier . . . won't there, darling?"

He turned her head back, feeling for the curve of her throat below the ear, and kissing her there, and on the hair and eyes and lips. She clung to him desperately, and as he drew her to his knees on the couch she felt as if they were being sucked down together into some bottomless abyss.

XV

That night, as usual, they said good-bye at the wood's edge.

Harney was to leave the next morning early. He asked Charity to say nothing of their plans till his return, and, strangely even to herself, she was glad of the postponement. A leaden weight of shame hung on her, benumbing every other sensation, and she bade him good-bye with hardly a sign of emotion. His reiterated promises to return seemed almost wounding. She had no doubt that he intended to come back; her doubts were far deeper and less definable.

Since the fanciful vision of the future that had flitted through her imagination at their first meeting she had hardly ever thought of his marrying her. She had not had to put the thought from her mind; it had not been there. If ever she looked ahead she felt instinctively that the gulf between them was too deep, and that the bridge their passion had flung across it was as insubstantial as a rainbow. But she seldom looked ahead; each day was so rich that it absorbed her. . . . Now her first feeling was that everything would be different, and that she herself would be a different being to Harney. Instead of remaining separate and absolute, she would be compared with other people, and unknown things would be expected of her. She was too proud to be afraid, but the freedom of her spirit drooped. . . .

Harney had not fixed any date for his return; he had said he would have to look about first, and settle things. He had promised to write as soon as there was anything definite to say, and had left her his address, and asked her to write also. But the address frightened her. It was in New York, at a club with a long name in Fifth Avenue: it seemed to raise an insurmountable barrier between them. Once or twice, in the first days, she got out a sheet of paper, and sat looking at it, and trying to think what to say; but she had the feeling that her letter would never reach its destination. She had never written to anyone farther away than Hepburn.

Harney's first letter came after he had been gone about ten days. It was tender but grave, and bore no resemblance to the gay little notes he had sent her by the freckled boy from Creston River. He spoke positively of his intention of coming back, but named no date, and reminded Charity of their agreement that their plans should not be divulged till he had had time to "settle things." When that would be he could not yet foresee; but she could count on his returning as soon as the way was clear.

She read the letter with a strange sense of its coming from immeasurable distances and having lost most of its meaning on the way; and in reply she sent him a coloured post-card of Creston Falls, on which she wrote: "With love from Charity." She felt the pitiful inadequacy of this, and understood, with a sense of despair, that in her inability to express herself she must give him an impression of coldness and reluctance; but she could not help it. She could not forget that he had never spoken to her of marriage till Mr. Royall had forced the word from his lips; though she had not had the strength to shake off the spell that bound her to him she had lost all spontaneity of feeling, and seemed to herself to be passively awaiting a fate she could not avert.

She had not seen Mr. Royall on her return to the red house. The morning after her parting from Harney, when she came down from her room, Verena told her that her guardian had gone off to Worcester and Portland. It was the time of year when he usually reported to the insurance agencies he represented, and there was nothing un- usual in his departure except its suddenness. She thought little about him, except to be glad he was not there. . . .

She kept to herself for the first days, while North Dormer was recovering from its brief plunge into publicity, and the subsiding agitation left her unnoticed. But the faithful Ally could not be long avoided. For the first few days after the close of the Old Home Week festivities Charity escaped her by roaming the hills all day when she was not at her post in the library; but after that a period of rain set in, and one pouring afternoon, Ally, sure that she would find her friend indoors, came around to the red house with her sewing.

The two girls sat upstairs in Charity's room. Charity, her idle hands in her lap, was sunk in a kind of leaden dream, through which she was only half-conscious of Ally, who sat opposite her in a low rush-bottomed chair, her work pinned to her knee, and her thin lips pursed up as she bent above it.

"It was my idea running a ribbon through the gauging," she said proudly, drawing back to contemplate the blouse she was trimming. "It's for Miss Balch: she was awfully pleased." She paused and then added, with a queer tremor in her piping voice: "I darsn't have told her I got the idea from one I saw on Julia."

Charity raised her eyes listlessly. "Do you

still see Julia sometimes?"

Ally reddened, as if the allusion had escaped her unintentionally. "Oh, it was a long time ago I seen her with those gaugings. . . ."

Silence fell again, and Ally presently continued: "Miss Balch left me a whole lot of things to do over this time."

"Why — has she gone?" Charity inquired with an inner start of apprehension.

"Didn't you know? She went off the morning after they had the celebration at Hamblin. I seen her drive by early with Mr. Harney."

There was another silence, measured by the steady tick of the rain against the window, and, at intervals, by the snipping sound of Ally's scissors.

Ally gave a meditative laugh. "Do you know what she told me before she went away? She told me she was going to send for me to come over to Springfield and make some things for her wedding."

Charity again lifted her heavy lids and stared at Ally's pale pointed face, which moved to and fro above her moving fingers.

"Is she going to get married?"

Ally let the blouse sink to her knee, and sat gazing at it. Her lips seemed suddenly dry, and she moistened them a little with her tongue.

"Why, I presume so . . . from what she

said. . . . Didn't you know?"

"Why should I know?"

Ally did not answer. She bent above the blouse, and began picking out a basting thread with the point of the scissors.

"Why should I know?" Charity repeated harshly.

"I didn't know but what . . . folks here say she's engaged to Mr. Harney."

Charity stood up with a laugh, and stretched her arms lazily above her head.

"If all the people got married that folks say are going to you'd have your time full making wedding dresses," she said ironically.

"Why — don't you believe it?" Ally ventured.

"It would not make it true if I did — nor prevent it if I didn't."

"That's so. . . . I only know I seen her crying the night of the party because her dress didn't set right. That was why she wouldn't dance any. . . ."

Charity stood absently gazing down at the lacy garment on Ally's knee. Abruptly she stooped and snatched it up.

"Well, I guess she won't dance in this either," she said with sudden violence; and grasping the blouse in her strong young hands she tore it in two and flung the tattered bits to the floor.

"Oh, Charity —" Ally cried, springing up.

For a long interval the two girls faced each other across the ruined garment. Ally burst into tears.

"Oh, what'll I say to her? What'll I do? It was real lace!" she wailed between her piping sobs.

Charity glared at her unrelentingly. "You'd oughtn't to have brought it here," she said, breathing quickly. "I hate other people's clothes — it's just as if they was there themselves." The two stared at each other again over this avowal, till Charity brought out, in a gasp of anguish: "Oh, go — go — go — or I'll hate you too. . . ."

When Ally left her, she fell sobbing across her bed.

The long storm was followed by a northwest gale, and when it was over, the hills took on their first umber tints, the sky grew more densely blue, and the big white clouds lay against the hills like snowbanks. The first crisp maple-leaves began to spin across Miss Hatchard's lawn, and the Virginia creeper on the Memorial splashed the white porch with scarlet. It was a golden triumphant September. Day by day the flame of the Virginia creeper spread to the hillsides in wider waves of carmine and crimson, the larches glowed like the thin yellow halo about a fire, the maples blazed and smouldered, and the black hemlocks turned to indigo against the incandescence of the forest.

The nights were cold, with a dry glitter of stars so high up that they seemed smaller and more vivid. Sometimes, as Charity lay sleepless on her bed through the long hours, she felt as though she were bound to those wheeling fires and swinging with them around the great black vault. At night she planned many things . . . it was then she wrote to Harney. But the letters were never put on paper, for she did not know how to express what she wanted to tell him. So she waited. Since her talk with Ally she had felt sure that Harney was engaged to Annabel Balch, and that the process of "settling things" would involve the breaking of this tie. Her first rage of jealousy over, she felt no fear on this score. She was still sure that Harney would come back, and she was equally sure that, for the moment at least, it was she whom he loved and not Miss Balch. Yet the girl, no less, remained a rival, since she represented all the things that Charity felt herself most incapable of understanding or achieving. Annabel Balch was, if not the girl Harney ought to marry, at least the kind of girl it would be natural for him to marry. Charity had never been able to picture herself as his wife; had never been able to arrest the vision and follow it out in its daily consequences; but she could perfectly imagine Annabel Balch in that relation to him.

The more she thought of these things the more the sense of fatality weighed on her: she felt the uselessness of struggling against the circumstances. She had never known how to adapt herself; she could only break and tear and destroy. The scene with Ally had left her stricken with shame at her own childish savagery. What would Harney have thought if he had witnessed it? But when she turned the incident over in her puzzled mind she could not imagine what a civilized person would have done in her place. She felt herself too unequally pitted against unknown forces. . . .

At length this feeling moved her to sudden action. She took a sheet of letter paper from Mr. Royall's office, and sitting by the kitchen lamp, one night after Verena had gone to bed, began her first letter to Harney. It was very short:

I want you should marry Annabel Balch if you promised to. I think maybe you were afraid I'd feel too bad about it. I feel I'd rather you acted right.
Your loving
CHARITY.

She posted the letter early the next morning, and for a few days her heart felt strangely light. Then she began to wonder why she received no answer.

One day as she sat alone in the library pondering these things the walls of books began to spin around her, and the rosewood desk to rock under her elbows. The dizziness was followed by a wave of nausea like that she had felt on the day of the exercises in the Town Hall. But the Town Hall had been crowded and stiflingly hot, and the library was empty, and so chilly that she had kept on her jacket. Five minutes before she had felt perfectly well; and now it seemed as if she were going to die. The bit of lace at which she still languidly worked dropped from her fingers, and the steel crochet hook clattered to the floor. She pressed her temples hard between her damp hands, steadying herself against the desk while the wave of sickness swept over her. Little by little it subsided, and after a few minutes she stood up, shaken and terrified, groped for her hat, and stumbled out into the air. But the whole sunlit autumn whirled, reeled and roared around her as she dragged herself along the interminable length of the road home.

As she approached the red house she saw a buggy standing at the door, and her heart gave a leap. But it was only Mr. Royall who got out, his travelling-bag in hand. He saw her coming, and waited on the porch. She was conscious that he was looking at her intently, as if there was something strange in her appearance, and she threw back her head with a desperate effort at ease. Their eyes met, and she said: "You back?" as if nothing had happened, and he answered: "Yes, I'm back," and walked in ahead of her, pushing open the door of his office. She climbed to her room, every step of the stairs holding her fast as if her feet were lined with glue.

Two days later, she descended from the train at Nettleton, and walked out of the station into the dusty square. The brief interval of cold weather was over, and the day was as soft, and almost as hot, as when she and Harney had emerged on the same scene on the Fourth of July. In the square the same broken-down hacks and carry-alls stood drawn up in a despondent line, and the lank horses with fly-nets over their withers swayed their heads drearily to and fro. She recognized the staring signs over the eating-houses and billiard saloons, and the long lines of wires on lofty poles taper-ing down the main street to the park at its other end. Taking the way the wires pointed, she went on hastily, with bent head, till she reached a wide transverse street with a brick building at the corner. She crossed this street and glanced furtively up at the front of the brick building; then she returned, and entered a door opening on a flight of steep brass-rimmed stairs. On the second landing she rang a bell, and a mulatto girl with a bushy head and a frilled apron let her into a hall where a stuffed fox on his hind legs proffered a brass card-tray to visitors. At the back of the hall was a glazed door marked: "Office." After waiting a few minutes in a handsomely furnished room, with plush sofas surmounted by large gold-framed photographs of showy young women, Charity was shown into the office. . . .

When she came out of the glazed door Dr. Merkle followed, and led her into another room, smaller, and still more crowded with plush and gold frames. Dr. Merkle was a plump woman with small bright eyes, an immense mass of black hair coming down low on her forehead, and unnaturally white and even teeth. She wore a rich black dress, with gold chains and charms hanging from her bosom. Her hands were large and smooth, and quick in all their movements; and she smelt of musk and carbolic acid.

She smiled on Charity with all her faultless teeth. "Sit down, my dear. Wouldn't you like a little drop of something to pick you up? . . . No. . . . Well, just lay back a minute then. . . . There's nothing to be done just yet; but in about a month, if you'll step round again . . . I could take you right into my own house for two or three days, and there wouldn't be a mite of trouble. Mercy me! The next time you'll know better'n to fret like this. . . ."

Charity gazed at her with widening eyes. This woman with the false hair, the false teeth, the false murderous smile — what was she offering her but immunity from some unthinkable crime? Charity, till then, had been conscious only of a vague self-disgust and a frightening physical distress; now, of a sudden, there came to her the grave surprise of motherhood. She had come to this dreadful place because she knew of no other way of making sure that she was not mistaken about her state; and the woman had taken her for a miserable creature like Julia. . . . The thought was so horrible that she sprang up, white and shaking, one of her great rushes of anger sweeping over her.

Dr. Merkle, still smiling, also rose. "Why do you run off in such a hurry? You can stretch out right here on my sofa. . . ." She paused, and her smile grew more motherly. "Afterwards — if there's been any talk at home, and you want to get away for a while . . . I have a lady friend in Boston who's looking for a companion . . . you're the very one to suit her, my dear. . . ."

Charity had reached the door. "I don't want to stay. I don't want to come back here," she stammered, her hand on the knob; but with a swift movement, Dr. Merkle edged her from the threshold.

"Oh, very well. Five dollars, please."

Charity looked helplessly at the doctor's tight lips and rigid face. Her last savings had gone in repaying Ally for the cost of Miss Balch's ruined blouse, and she had had to borrow four dollars from her friend to pay for her railway ticket and cover the doctor's fee. It had never occurred to her that medical advice could cost more than two dollars.

"I didn't know . . . I haven't got that much . . ." she faltered, bursting into tears.

Dr. Merkle gave a short laugh which did not show her teeth and inquired with concision if Charity supposed she ran the establishment for her own amusement? She leaned her firm shoulders against the door as she spoke, like a grim gaoler making terms with her captive.

"You say you'll come round and settle later? I've heard that pretty often too. Give me your address, and if you can't pay me I'll send the bill to your folks. . . . What? I can't understand what you say. . . . That don't suit you neither? My, you're pretty particular for a girl that ain't got enough to settle her own bills. . . ." She paused, and fixed her eyes on the brooch with a blue stone that Charity had pinned to her blouse.

"Ain't you ashamed to talk that way to a lady that's got to earn her living, when you go about with jewellery like that on you? . . . It ain't in my line, and I do it only as a favour . . . but if you're a mind to leave that brooch as a pledge, I don't say no. . . . Yes, of course, you can get it back when you bring me my money. . . ."

On the way home, she felt an immense and unexpected quietude. It had been horrible to have to leave Harney's gift in the woman's hands, but even at that price the news she brought away had not been too dearly bought. She sat with half-closed eyes as the train rushed through the familiar landscape; and now the memories of her former journey, instead of flying before her like dead leaves, seemed to be ripening in her blood like sleeping grain. She would never again know what it was to feel herself alone. Everything seemed to have grown suddenly clear and simple. She no longer had any difficulty in picturing herself as Harney's wife now that she was the mother of his child; and compared to her sovereign right Annabel Balch's claim seemed no more than a girl's sentimental fancy.

That evening, at the gate of the red house, she found Ally waiting in the dusk. "I was down at the post-office just as they were closing up, and Will Targatt said there was a letter for you, so I brought it."

Ally held out the letter, looking at Charity with piercing sympathy. Since the scene of the torn blouse there had been a new and fearful admiration in the eyes she bent on her friend.

Charity snatched the letter with a laugh. "Oh, thank you — good-night," she called out over her shoulder as she ran up the path. If she had lingered a moment she knew she would have had Ally at her heels.

She hurried upstairs and felt her way into her dark room. Her hands trembled as she groped for the matches and lit her candle, and the flap of the envelope was so closely stuck that she had to find her scissors and slit it open. At length she read:

DEAR CHARITY:

I have your letter, and it touches me more than I can say. Won't you trust me, in return, to do my best? There are things it is hard to explain, much less to justify; but your generosity makes everything easier. All I can do now is to thank you from my soul for under-standing. Your telling me that you

207

wanted me to do right has helped me beyond expression. If ever there is a hope of realizing what we dreamed of you will see me back on the instant; and I haven't yet lost that hope.

She read the letter with a rush; then she went over and over it, each time more slowly and painstakingly. It was so beautifully expressed that she found it almost as difficult to understand as the gentleman's explanation of the Bible pictures at Nettleton; but gradually she became aware that the gist of its meaning lay in the last few words. "If ever there is a hope of realizing what we dreamed of . . ."

But then he wasn't even sure of that? She understood now that every word and every reticence was an avowal of Annabel Balch's prior claim. It was true that he was engaged to her, and that he had not yet found a way of breaking his engagement.

As she read the letter over Charity understood what it must have cost him to write it. He was not trying to evade an importunate claim; he was honestly and contritely struggling between opposing duties. She did not even reproach him in her thoughts for having concealed from her that he was not free: she could not see anything more reprehensible in his conduct than in her own. From the first she had needed him more than he had wanted her, and the power that had swept them together had been as far beyond resistance as a great gale loosening the leaves of the forest. . . . Only, there stood between them, fixed and upright in the general upheaval, the indestructible figure of Annabel Balch. . . .

Face to face with his admission of the fact, she sat staring at the letter. A cold tremor ran over her, and the hard sobs struggled up into her throat and shook her from head to foot. For a while she was caught and tossed on great waves of anguish that left her hardly conscious of anything but the blind struggle against their assaults. Then, little by little, she began to relive, with a dreadful poignancy, each separate stage of her poor romance. Foolish things she had said came back to her, gay answers Harney had made, his first kiss in the darkness between the fireworks, their choosing the blue brooch together, the way he had teased her about the letters she had dropped in her flight from the evangelist. All these memories, and a thousand others, hummed through her brain till his nearness grew so vivid that she felt his fingers in her hair, and his warm breath on her cheek as he bent her head back like a flower. These things were hers; they had passed into her blood, and become a part of her, they were building the child in her womb; it was impossible to tear asunder strands of life so interwoven.

The conviction gradually strengthened her, and she began to form in her mind the first words of the letter she meant to write to Harney. She wanted to write it at once, and with feverish hands she began to rummage in her drawer for a sheet of letter-paper. But there was none left; she must go downstairs to get it. She had a superstitious feeling that the letter must be written on the instant, that setting down her secrets in words would bring her reassurance and safety; and taking up her candle she went down to Mr. Royall's office.

At that hour she was not likely to find him there: he had probably had his supper and walked over to Carrick Fry's. She pushed open the door of the unlit room, and the light of her lifted candle fell on his figure, seated in the darkness in his high-backed chair. His arms lay along the arms of the chair, and his head was bent a little; but he lifted it quickly as Charity entered. She started back as their eyes met, remembering that her own were red with weeping, and that her face was livid with the fatigue and emotion of her journey. But it was too late to escape, and she stood and looked at him in silence.

He had risen from his chair, and came toward her with outstretched hands. The gesture was so unexpected that she let him take her hands in his and they stood thus, without speaking, till Mr. Royall said gravely: "Charity — was you looking for me?"

She freed herself abruptly and fell back. "Me? No —" She set down the candle on his desk. "I wanted some letter-paper, that's all."

His face contracted, and the bushy brows jutted forward over his eyes. Without answering he opened the drawer of the desk, took out a sheet of paper and an envelope, and pushed them toward her. "Do you want a stamp too?" he asked.

She nodded, and he gave her the stamp. As he did so she felt that he was looking at her intently, and she knew that the candle light flickering up on her white face must be distorting her swollen features and exaggerating the dark rings about her eyes. She snatched up the paper, her reassurance dissolving under his pitiless gaze, in which she seemed to read the grim perception of her state, and the ironic recollection of the day when, in that very room, he had offered to compel Harney to marry her. His look seemed to say that he knew she had taken the paper to write to her lover, who had left her as he had warned her she would be left. She remembered the scorn with which she had turned from him that day, and knew, if he guessed the truth, what a list of old scores it must settle. She turned and fled upstairs; but when she got back to her room all the words that had been waiting had vanished. . . .

If she could have gone to Harney it would have been different; she would only have had to show herself to let his memories speak for her. But she had no money left, and there was no one from whom she could have borrowed enough for such a journey. There was nothing to do but to write, and await his reply. For a long time she sat bent above the blank page; but she found nothing to say that really expressed what she was feeling. . . .

Harney had written that she had made it easier for him, and she was glad it was so; she did not want to make things hard. She knew she had it in her power to do that; she held his fate in her hands. All she had to do was to tell him the truth; but that was the very fact that held her back. . . . Her five minutes face to face with Mr. Royall had stripped her of her last illusion, and brought her back to North Dormer's point of view. Distinctly and pitilessly there rose before her the fate of the girl who was married "to make things right." She had seen too many village love-stories end in that way. Poor Rose Coles's miserable marriage was of the number; and what good had come of it for her or for Halston Skeff? They had hated each other from the day the minister married them; and whenever old Mrs. Skeff had a fancy to humiliate her daughter-in-law she had only to say: "Who'd ever think the baby's only two? And for a seven months' child — ain't it a wonder what a size he is?" North Dormer had treasures of indulgence for brands in the burning, but only derision for those who succeeded in getting snatched from it; and Charity had always understood Julia Hawes's refusal to be snatched. . . .

Only — was there no alternative but Julia's? Her soul recoiled from the vision of the white-faced woman among the plush sofas and gilt frames. In the established order of things as she knew them she saw no place for her individual adventure. . . .

She sat in her chair without undressing till faint grey streaks began to divide the black slats of the shutters. Then she stood up and pushed them open, letting in the light. The coming of a new day brought a sharper consciousness of ineluctable reality, and with it a sense of the need of action. She looked at herself in the glass, and saw her face: white in the autumn dawn, with pinched cheeks and dark-ringed eyes, and all the marks of her state that she herself would never have noticed, but that Dr. Merkle's diagnosis had made plain to her.

She could not hope that those signs would escape the watchful village; even before her figure lost its shape she knew her face would betray her.

Leaning from her window she looked out on the dark and empty scene; the ashen houses with shuttered windows, the grey road climbing the slope to the hemlock belt above the cemetery, and the heavy mass of the Mountain black against a rainy sky. To the east a space of light was broadening above the forest; but over that also the clouds hung. Slowly her gaze travelled across the fields to the rugged curve of the hills. She had looked out so often on that lifeless circle, and wondered if anything could ever happen to anyone who was enclosed in it. . . .

Almost without conscious thought her decision had been reached; as her eyes had followed the circle of the hills her mind had also travelled the old round. She supposed it was something in her blood that made the Mountain the only answer to her questioning, the inevitable escape from all that hemmed her in and beset her. At any rate it began to loom against the rainy dawn; and the longer she looked at it the more clearly she understood that now at last she was really going there.

XVI

The rain held off, and an hour later, when she started, wild gleams of sunlight were blowing across the fields.

After Harney's departure she had returned her bicycle to its owner at Creston, and she was not sure of being able to walk all the way to the Mountain. The deserted house was on the road; but the idea of spending the night there was unendurable, and she meant to try to push on to Hamblin, where she could sleep under a wood-shed if her strength should fail her. Her preparations had been made with quiet forethought. Before starting she had forced herself to swallow a glass of milk and eat a piece of bread; and she had put in her canvas satchel a little packet of the chocolate that Harney always carried in his bicycle bag. She wanted above all to keep up her strength, and reach her destination without attracting notice. . . .

Mile by mile she retraced the road over which she had so often flown to her lover. When she reached the turn where the wood-road branched off from the Creston highway she remembered the Gospel tent — long since folded up and transplanted — and her start of involuntary terror when the fat evangelist had said: "Your Saviour knows everything. Come and confess your guilt." There was no sense of guilt in her now, but only a desperate desire to defend her secret from irreverent eyes, and begin life again among people to whom the harsh code of the village was unknown. The impulse did not shape itself in thought: she only knew she must save her baby, and hide herself with it somewhere where no one would ever come to trouble them.

She walked on and on, growing more heavy-footed as the day advanced. It seemed a cruel chance that compelled her to retrace every step of the way to the deserted house; and when she came in sight of the orchard, and the silver-grey roof slanting crookedly through the laden branches, her strength failed her and she sat down by the roadside. She sat there a long time, trying to gather the courage to start again, and walk past the broken gate and the untrimmed rose-bushes strung with scarlet hips. A few drops of rain were falling, and she thought of the warm evenings when she and Harney had sat embraced in the shadowy room, and the noise of summer showers on the roof had rustled through their kisses. At length she understood that if she stayed any longer the rain might compel her to take shelter in the house overnight, and she got up and walked on, averting her eyes as she came abreast of the white gate and the tangled garden.

The hours wore on, and she walked more and more slowly, pausing now and then to rest, and to eat a little bread and an apple picked up from the roadside. Her body seemed to grow heavier with every yard of the way, and she wondered how she would be able to carry her child later, if already he laid such a burden on her. . . . A fresh wind had sprung up, scattering the rain and blowing down keenly from the mountain. Presently the clouds lowered again, and a few white darts struck her in the face: it was the first snow falling over Hamblin. The roofs of the lonely village were only half a mile ahead, and she was resolved to push beyond it, and try to reach the Mountain that night. She had no clear plan of action, except that, once in the settlement, she meant to look for Liff Hyatt, and get him to take her to her mother. She herself had been born as her own baby was going to be born; and whatever her mother's subsequent life had been, she could hardly help remembering the past, and receiving a daughter who was facing the trouble she had known.

Suddenly the deadly faintness came over her once more and she sat down on the bank and leaned her head against a tree-trunk. The long road and the cloudy land-scape vanished from her eyes, and for a time she seemed to be circling about in some terrible wheeling darkness. Then that too faded.

She opened her eyes, and saw a buggy drawn up beside her, and a man who had jumped down from it and was gazing at her with a puzzled face. Slowly consciousness came back, and she saw that the man was Liff Hyatt.

She was dimly aware that he was asking her something, and she looked at him in silence, trying to find strength to speak. At length her voice stirred in her throat, and she said in a whisper: "I'm going up the Mountain."

"Up the Mountain?" he repeated, drawing aside a little; and as he moved she saw behind him, in the buggy, a heavily coated figure with a familiar pink face and gold spectacles on the bridge of a Grecian nose.

"Charity! What on earth are you doing here?" Mr. Miles exclaimed, throwing the reins on the horse's back and scrambling down from the buggy.

She lifted her heavy eyes to his. "I'm going to see my mother."

The two men glanced at each other, and

for a moment neither of them spoke.

Then Mr. Miles said: "You look ill, my dear, and it's a long way. Do you think it's wise?"

Charity stood up. "I've got to go to her."

A vague mirthless grin contracted Liff Hyatt's face, and Mr. Miles again spoke uncertainly. "You know, then — you'd been told?"

She stared at him. "I don't know what you mean. I want to go to her."

Mr. Miles was examining her thoughtfully. She fancied she saw a change in his expression, and the blood rushed to her forehead. "I just want to go to her," she repeated.

He laid his hand on her arm. "My child, your mother is dying. Liff Hyatt came down to fetch me. . . . Get in and come with us."

He helped her up to the seat at his side, Liff Hyatt clambered in at the back, and they drove off toward Hamblin. At first Charity had hardly grasped what Mr. Miles was saying; the physical relief of finding herself seated in the buggy, and securely on her road to the Mountain, effaced the impression of his words. But as her head cleared she began to understand. She knew the Mountain had but the most infrequent intercourse with the valleys; she had often enough heard it said that no one ever went up there except the minister, when someone was dying. And now it was her mother who was dying . . . and she would find herself as much alone on the Mountain as anywhere else in the world. The sense of unescapable isolation was all she could feel for the moment; then she began to wonder at the strangeness of its being Mr. Miles who had undertaken to perform this grim errand. He did not seem in the least like the kind of man who would care to go up the Mountain. But here he was at her side, guiding the horse with a firm hand, and bending on her the kindly gleam of his spectacles, as if there were nothing un-usual in their being together in such cir-cumstances.

For a while she found it impossible to speak, and he seemed to understand this, and made no attempt to question her. But presently she felt her tears rise and flow down over her drawn cheeks; and he must have seen them too, for he laid his hand on hers, and said in a low voice: "Won't you tell me what is troubling you?"

She shook her head, and he did not insist: but after a while he said, in the same low tone, so that they should not be overheard: "Charity, what do you know of your child-hood, before you came down to North Dor-mer?"

She controlled herself, and answered: "Nothing only what I heard Mr. Royall say one day. He said he brought me down because my father went to prison."

"And you've never been up there since?"

"Never."

Mr. Miles was silent again, then he said: "I'm glad you're coming with me now. Perhaps we may find your mother alive, and she may know that you have come."

They had reached Hamblin, where the snow-flurry had left white patches in the rough grass on the roadside, and in the angles of the roofs facing north. It was a poor bleak village under the granite flank of the Mountain, and as soon as they left it they began to climb. The road was steep and full of ruts, and the horse settled down to a walk while they mounted and mounted, the world dropping away below them in great mottled stretches of forest and field, and stormy dark blue distances.

Charity had often had visions of this ascent of the Mountain but she had not known it would reveal so wide a country, and the sight of those strange lands reaching away on every side gave her a new sense of Harney's remoteness. She knew he must be miles and miles beyond the last range of hills that seemed to be the outmost verge of things, and she wondered how she had ever dreamed of going to New York to find him. . . .

As the road mounted the country grew

bleaker, and they drove across fields of faded mountain grass bleached by long months beneath the snow. In the hollows a few white birches trembled, or a mountain ash lit its scarlet clusters; but only a scant growth of pines darkened the granite ledges. The wind was blowing fiercely across the open slopes; the horse faced it with bent head and straining flanks, and now and then the buggy swayed so that Charity had to clutch its side.

Mr. Miles had not spoken again; he seemed to understand that she wanted to be left alone. After a while the track they were following forked, and he pulled up the horse, as if uncertain of the way. Liff Hyatt craned his head around from the back, and shouted against the wind: "Left —" and they turned into a stunted pine-wood and began to drive down the other side of the Mountain.

A mile or two farther on they came out on a clearing where two or three low houses lay in stony fields, crouching among the rocks as if to brace themselves against the wind. They were hardly more than sheds, built of logs and rough boards, with tin stove-pipes sticking out of their roofs. The sun was setting, and dusk had already fallen on the lower world, but a yellow glare still lay on the lonely hillside and the crouching houses. The next moment it faded and left the landscape in dark autumn twilight.

"Over there," Liff called out, stretching his long arm over Mr. Miles's shoulder. The clergyman turned to the left, across a bit of bare ground overgrown with docks and nettles, and stopped before the most ruinous of the sheds. A stove-pipe reached its crooked arm out of one window, and the broken panes of the other were stuffed with rags and paper. In contrast to such a dwelling the brown house in the swamp might have stood for the home of plenty.

As the buggy drew up two or three mongrel dogs jumped out of the twilight with a great barking, and a young man slouched to the door and stood there staring. In the twilight Charity saw that his face had the same sodden look as Bash Hyatt's, the day she had seen him sleeping by the stove. He made no effort to silence the dogs, but leaned in the door, as if roused from a drunken lethargy, while Mr. Miles got out of the buggy.

"Is it here?" the clergyman asked Liff in a low voice; and Liff nodded.

Mr. Miles turned to Charity. "Just hold the horse a minute, my dear: I'll go in first," he said, putting the reins in her hands. She took them passively, and sat staring straight ahead of her at the darkening scene while Mr. Miles and Liff Hyatt went

223

up to the house. They stood a few minutes talking with the man in the door, and then Mr. Miles came back. As he came close, Charity saw that his smooth pink face wore a frightened solemn look.

"Your mother is dead, Charity; you'd better come with me," he said.

She got down and followed him while Liff led the horse away. As she approached the door she said to herself: "This is where I was born . . . this is where I belong. . . ." She had said it to herself often enough as she looked across the sunlit valleys at the Mountain; but it had meant nothing then, and now it had become a reality. Mr. Miles took her gently by the arm, and they entered what appeared to be the only room in the house. It was so dark that she could just discern a group of a dozen people sitting or sprawling about a table made of boards laid across two barrels. They looked up listlessly as Mr. Miles and Charity came in, and a woman's thick voice said: "Here's the preacher." But no one moved.

Mr. Miles paused and looked about him; then he turned to the young man who had met them at the door.

"Is the body here?" he asked.

The young man, instead of answering, turned his head toward the group. "Where's the candle? I tole yer to bring a candle," he said with sudden harshness to a girl who

224

was lolling against the table. She did not answer, but another man got up and took from some corner a candle stuck into a bottle.

"How'll I light it? The stove's out," the girl grumbled.

Mr. Miles fumbled under his heavy wrappings and drew out a match-box. He held a match to the candle, and in a moment or two a faint circle of light fell on the pale aguish heads that started out of the shadow like the heads of nocturnal animals.

"Mary's over there," someone said; and Mr. Miles, taking the bottle in his hand, passed behind the table. Charity followed him, and they stood before a mattress on the floor in a corner of the room. A woman lay on it, but she did not look like a dead woman; she seemed to have fallen across her squalid bed in a drunken sleep, and to have been left lying where she fell, in her ragged disordered clothes. One arm was flung above her head, one leg drawn up under a torn skirt that left the other bare to the knee: a swollen glistening leg with a ragged stocking rolled down about the ankle. The woman lay on her back, her eyes staring up unblinkingly at the candle that trembled in Mr. Miles's hand.

"She jus' dropped off," a woman said, over the shoulder of the others; and the young man added: "I jus' come in and found her."

An elderly man with lank hair and a feeble grin pushed between them. "It was like this: I says to her on'y the night before: if you don't take and quit, I says to her . . ."

Someone pulled him back and sent him reeling against a bench along the wall, where he dropped down muttering his un-heeded narrative.

There was a silence; then the young woman who had been lolling against the table suddenly parted the group, and stood in front of Charity. She was healthier and robuster looking than the others, and her weather-beaten face had a certain sullen beauty.

"Who's the girl? Who brought her here?" she said, fixing her eyes mistrustfully on the young man who had rebuked her for not having a candle ready.

Mr. Miles spoke. "I brought her; she is Mary Hyatt's daughter."

"What? Her too?" the girl sneered; and the young man turned on her with an oath. "Shut your mouth, damn you, or get out of here," he said; then he relapsed into his former apathy, and dropped down on the bench, leaning his head against the wall.

Mr. Miles had set the candle on the floor and taken off his heavy coat. He turned to Charity. "Come and help me," he said.

He knelt down by the mattress, and pressed the lids over the dead woman's eyes. Charity, trembling and sick, knelt beside him, and tried to compose her mother's body. She drew the stocking over the dreadful glistening leg, and pulled the skirt down to the battered upturned boots. As she did so, she looked at her mother's face, thin yet swollen, with lips parted in a frozen gasp above the broken teeth. There was no sign in it of anything human: she lay there like a dead dog in a ditch. Charity's hands grew cold as they touched her.

Mr. Miles drew the woman's arms across her breast and laid his coat over her. Then he covered her face with his handkerchief, and placed the bottle with the candle in it at her head. Having done this he stood up.

"Is there no coffin?" he asked, turning to the group behind him.

There was a moment of bewildered silence; then the fierce girl spoke up. "You'd oughter brought it with you. Where'd we get one here, I'd like ter know?"

Mr. Miles, looking at the others, repeated: "Is it possible you have no coffin ready?"

"That's what I say: them that has it sleeps better," an old woman murmured. "But then she never had no bed. . . ."

"And the stove warn't hers," said the lank-haired man, on the defensive.

Mr. Miles turned away from them and moved a few steps apart. He had drawn a book from his pocket, and after a pause he

227

opened it and began to read, holding the book at arm's length and low down, so that the pages caught the feeble light. Charity had remained on her knees by the mattress: now that her mother's face was covered it was easier to stay near her, and avoid the sight of the living faces which too horribly showed by what stages hers had lapsed into death.

"I am the Resurrection and the Life," Mr. Miles began; "he that believeth in me, though he were dead, yet shall he live. . . . Though after my skin worms destroy my body, yet in my flesh shall I see God. . . ."

In my flesh shall I see God! Charity thought of the gaping mouth and stony eyes under the handkerchief, and of the glistening leg over which she had drawn the stocking. . . .

"We brought nothing into this world and we shall take nothing out of it —"

There was a sudden muttering and a scuffle at the back of the group. "I brought the stove," said the elderly man with lank hair, pushing his way between the others. "I wen' down to Creston'n bought it . . . n' I got a right to take it outer here . . . n' I'll lick any feller says I ain't. . . ."

"Sit down, damn you!" shouted the tall youth who had been drowsing on the bench against the wall.

"For man walketh in a vain shadow, and

disquieteth himself in vain; he heapeth up riches and cannot tell who shall gather them . . ."

"Well, it *are* his," a woman in the background interjected in a frightened whine.

The tall youth staggered to his feet. "If you don't hold your mouths I'll turn you all out o' here, the whole lot of you," he cried with many oaths. "G'wan, minister . . . don't let 'em faze you. . . ."

"Now is Christ risen from the dead and become the first-fruits of them that slept. . . . Behold, I show you a mystery. We shall not all sleep, but we shall all be changed, in a moment, in the twinkling of an eye, at the last trump. . . . For this corruptible must put on incorruption and this mortal must put on immortality. So when this corruption shall have put on incorruption, and when this mortal shall have put on immortality, then shall be brought to pass the saying that is written, Death is swallowed up in Victory. . . ."

One by one the mighty words fell on Charity's bowed head, soothing the horror, subduing the tumult, mastering her as they mastered the drink-dazed creatures at her back. Mr. Miles read to the last word, and then closed the book.

"Is the grave ready?" he asked.

Liff Hyatt, who had come in while he was reading, nodded a "Yes," and pushed forward to the side of the mattress. The young man on the bench who seemed to assert some sort of right of kinship with the dead woman, got to his feet again, and the proprietor of the stove joined him. Between them they raised up the mattress; but their movements were unsteady, and the coat slipped to the floor, revealing the poor body in its helpless misery. Charity, picking up the coat, covered her mother once more. Liff had brought a lantern, and the old woman who had already spoken took it up, and opened the door to let the little procession pass out. The wind had dropped, and the night was very dark and bitterly cold. The old woman walked ahead, the lantern shaking in her hand and spreading out before her a pale patch of dead grass and coarse-leaved weeds enclosed in an immensity of blackness.

Mr. Miles took Charity by the arm, and side by side they walked behind the mattress. At length the old woman with the lantern stopped, and Charity saw the light fall on the stooping shoulders of the bearers and on a ridge of upheaved earth over which they were bending. Mr. Miles released her arm and approached the hollow on the other side of the ridge; and while the men stooped down, lowering the mattress into the grave, he began to speak again.

"Man that is born of woman hath but a

short time to live and is full of misery. . . . He cometh up and is cut down . . . he fleeth as it were a shadow. . . . Yet, O Lord God most holy, O Lord most mighty, O holy and merciful Saviour, deliver us not into the bitter pains of eternal death . . ."

"Easy there . . . is she down?" piped the claimant to the stove; and the young man called over his shoulder: "Lift the light there, can't you?"

There was a pause, during which the light floated uncertainly over the open grave. Someone bent over and pulled out Mr. Miles's coat — ("No, no — leave the hand-kerchief," he interposed) — and then Liff Hyatt, coming forward with a spade, began to shovel in the earth.

"Forasmuch as it hath pleased Almighty God of His great mercy to take unto Himself the soul of our dear sister here departed, we therefore commit her body to the ground; earth to earth, ashes to ashes, dust to dust . . ." Liff's gaunt shoulders rose and bent in the lantern light as he dashed the clods of earth into the grave. "God — it's froze a'ready," he muttered, spitting into his palm and passing his ragged shirt-sleeve across his perspiring face.

"Through our Lord Jesus Christ, who shall change our vile body that it may be like unto His glorious body, according to the mighty working, whereby He is able to subdue all things unto Himself . . ." The last spadeful of earth fell on the vile body of Mary Hyatt, and Liff rested on his spade, his shoulder blades still heaving with the effort.

"Lord, have mercy upon us, Christ have mercy upon us, Lord have mercy upon us. . . ."

Mr. Miles took the lantern from the old woman's hand and swept its light across the circle of bleared faces. "Now kneel down, all of you," he commanded, in a voice of authority that Charity had never heard. She knelt down at the edge of the grave, and the others, stiffly and hesitatingly, got to their knees beside her. Mr. Miles knelt, too. "And now pray with me — you know this prayer," he said, and he began: "Our Father which art in Heaven . . ." One or two of the women falteringly took the words up, and when he ended, the lank-haired man flung himself on the neck of the tall youth. "It was this way," he said. "I tole her the night before, I says to her . . ." The reminiscence ended in a sob.

Mr. Miles had been getting into his coat again. He came up to Charity, who had remained passively kneeling by the rough mound of earth.

"My child, you must come. It's very late."

She lifted her eyes to his face: he seemed to speak out of another world.

"I ain't coming: I'm going to stay here."

"Here? Where? What do you mean?"

"These are my folks. I'm going to stay with them."

Mr. Miles lowered his voice. "But it's not possible — you don't know what you are doing. You can't stay among these people: you must come with me."

She shook her head and rose from her knees. The group about the grave had scattered in the darkness, but the old woman with the lantern stood waiting. Her mournful withered face was not unkind, and Charity went up to her.

"Have you got a place where I can lie down for the night?" she asked. Liff came up, leading the buggy out of the night. He looked from one to the other with his feeble smile. "She's my mother. She'll take you home," he said; and he added, raising his voice to speak to the old woman: "It's the girl from lawyer Royall's — Mary's girl . . . you remember. . . ."

The woman nodded and raised her sad old eyes to Charity's. When Mr. Miles and Liff clambered into the buggy she went ahead with the lantern to show them the track they were to follow; then she turned back, and in silence she and Charity walked away together through the night.

XVII

Charity lay on the floor on a mattress, as her dead mother's body had lain. The room in which she lay was cold and dark and low-ceilinged, and even poorer and barer than the scene of Mary Hyatt's earthly pilgrimage. On the other side of the fireless stove Liff Hyatt's mother slept on a blanket, with two children — her grandchildren, she said — rolled up against her like sleeping puppies. They had their thin clothes spread over them, having given the only other blanket to their guest.

Through the small square of glass in the opposite wall Charity saw a deep funnel of sky, so black, so remote, so palpitating with frosty stars that her very soul seemed to be sucked into it. Up there somewhere, she supposed, the God whom Mr. Miles had invoked was waiting for Mary Hyatt to appear. What a long flight it was! And what would she have to say when she reached Him?

Charity's bewildered brain laboured with the attempt to picture her mother's past, and to relate it in any way to the designs of a just but merciful God; but it was impossible to imagine any link between them. She herself felt as remote from the poor creature she had seen lowered into her hastily dug grave as if the height of the heavens divided them. She had seen poverty and misfortune in her life; but in a community where poor thrifty Mrs. Hawes and the industrious Ally represented the nearest approach to destitution there was nothing to suggest the savage misery of the Mountain farmers.

As she lay there, half-stunned by her tragic initiation, Charity vainly tried to think herself into the life about her. But she could not even make out what relationship these people bore to each other, or to her dead mother; they seemed to be herded together in a sort of passive promiscuity in which their common misery was the strongest link. She tried to picture to herself what her life would have been if she had grown up on the Mountain, running wild in rags, sleeping on the floor curled up against her mother, like the pale-faced children huddled against old Mrs. Hyatt, and turning into a fierce bewildered creature like the girl who had apostrophized her in such strange words. She was frightened by the secret affinity she had felt with this girl, and by the light it threw on her own beginnings. Then she remembered what Mr. Royall had said in telling her story to Lucius Harney: "Yes, there was a mother; but she was glad to have the child go. She'd have given her to anybody. . . ."

Well! after all, was her mother so much to blame? Charity, since that day, had always thought of her as destitute of all human feeling; now she seemed merely pitiful. What mother would not want to save her child from such a life? Charity thought of the future of her own child, and tears welled into her aching eyes, and ran down over her face. If she had been less exhausted, less burdened with his weight, she would have sprung up then and there and fled away. . . .

The grim hours of the night dragged themselves slowly by, and at last the sky paled and dawn threw a cold blue beam into the room. She lay in her corner staring at the dirty floor, the clothes-line hung with decaying rags, the old woman huddled against the cold stove, and the light gradually spreading across the wintry world, and bringing with it a new day in which she would have to live, to choose, to act, to make herself a place among these people — or to go back to the life she had left. A mortal lassitude weighed on her. There were moments when she felt that all she asked was to go on lying there unnoticed; then her mind revolted at the thought of becoming one of the miserable herd from which she sprang, and it seemed as though, to save her child from such a fate, she would find strength to travel any distance, and bear any burden life might put on her.

Vague thoughts of Nettleton flitted through her mind. She said to herself that she would find some quiet place where she could bear her child, and give it to decent people to keep; and then she would go out like Julia Hawes and earn its living and hers. She knew that girls of that kind sometimes made enough to have their children nicely cared for; and every other consideration disappeared in the vision of her baby, cleaned and combed and rosy, and hidden away somewhere where she could run in and kiss it, and bring it pretty things to wear. Anything, anything was better than to add another life to the nest of misery on the Mountain. . . .

The old woman and the children were still sleeping when Charity rose from her mattress. Her body was stiff with cold and fatigue, and she moved slowly lest her heavy steps should rouse them. She was faint with hunger, and had nothing left in her satchel; but on the table she saw the half of a stale loaf. No doubt it was to serve as the breakfast of old Mrs. Hyatt and the children; but Charity did not care; she had her own baby to think of. She broke off a piece of the bread and ate it greedily; then her glance fell on the thin faces of the sleeping children, and filled with compunction she rummaged in her satchel for something with which to pay for what she had taken. She found one of the pretty chemises that Ally had made for her, with a blue ribbon run through its edging. It was one of the dainty things on which she had squandered her savings, and as she looked at it the blood rushed to her forehead. She laid the chemise on the table, and stealing across the floor lifted the latch and went out. . . .

The morning was icy cold and a pale sun was just rising above the eastern shoulder of the Mountain. The houses scattered on the hillside lay cold and smokeless under the sun-flecked clouds, and not a human being was in sight. Charity paused on the threshold and tried to discover the road by which she had come the night before. Across the field surrounding Mrs. Hyatt's shanty she saw the tumble-down house in which she supposed the funeral service had taken place. The trail ran across the ground between the two houses and disappeared in the pine-wood on the flank of the Mountain; and a little way to the right, under a wind-beaten thorn, a mound of fresh earth made a dark spot on the fawn-coloured stubble. Charity walked across the field to the ground. As she approached it she heard a bird's note in the still air, and looking up she saw a brown song-sparrow perched in an upper branch of the thorn above the grave. She stood a minute listening to his small solitary song; then she rejoined the trail and began to mount the hill to the pine-wood.

Thus far she had been impelled by the blind instinct of flight; but each step seemed to bring her nearer to the realities of which her feverish vigil had given only a shadowy image. Now that she walked again in a daylight world, on the way back to familiar things, her imagination moved more soberly. On one point she was still decided: she could not remain at North Dormer, and the sooner she got away from it the better. But everything beyond was darkness.

As she continued to climb the air grew keener, and when she passed from the shelter of the pines to the open grassy roof of the Mountain the cold wind of the night before sprang out on her. She bent her shoulders and struggled on against it for a while; but presently her breath failed, and she sat down under a ledge of rock over-hung by shivering birches. From where she sat she saw the trail wandering across the bleached grass in the direction of Hamblin, and the granite wall of the Mountain falling away to infinite distances. On that side of the ridge the valleys still lay in wintry shadow; but in the plain beyond the sun was touching village roofs and steeples, and gilding the haze of smoke over far-off invisible towns.

Charity felt herself a mere speck in the lonely circle of the sky. The events of the last two days seemed to have divided her forever from her short dream of bliss. Even Harney's image had been blurred by that crushing experience: she thought of him as so remote from her that he seemed hardly more than a memory. In her fagged and floating mind only one sensation had the weight of reality; it was the bodily burden of her child. But for it she would have felt as rootless as the whiffs of thistledown the wind blew past her. Her child was like a load that held her down, and yet like a hand that pulled her to her feet. She said to herself that she must get up and struggle on. . . .

Her eyes turned back to the trail across the top of the Mountain, and in the distance she saw a buggy against the sky. She knew its antique outline, and the gaunt build of the old horse pressing forward with lowered head; and after a moment she recognized the heavy bulk of the man who held the reins. The buggy was following the trail and making straight for the pine-wood through which she had climbed; and she knew at once that the driver was in search of her. Her first impulse was to crouch down under the ledge till he had passed; but the instinct of concealment was overruled by the relief of feeling that someone was near her in the awful emptiness. She stood up and walked toward the buggy.

Mr. Royall saw her, and touched the horse with the whip. A minute or two later he was abreast of Charity; their eyes met, and without speaking he leaned over and helped her up into the buggy. She tried to speak, to stammer out some explanation, but no words came to her; and as he drew the cover over her knees he simply said: "The minister told me he'd left you up here, so I come up for you."

He turned the horse's head, and they began to jog back toward Hamblin. Charity sat speechless, staring straight ahead of her, and Mr. Royall occasionally uttered a word of encouragement to the horse. "Get along there, Dan. . . . I gave him a rest at Hamblin; but I brought him along pretty quick, and it's a stiff pull up here against the wind."

As he spoke it occurred to her for the first time that to reach the top of the Mountain so early he must have left North Dormer at the coldest hour of the night, and have travelled steadily but for the halt at Hamblin; and she felt a softness at her heart which no act of his had ever produced since he had brought her the Crimson Rambler because she had given up boarding-school to stay with him.

After an interval he began again: "It was a day just like this, only spitting snow, when I come up here for you the first time." Then, as if fearing that she might take his remark as a reminder of past benefits, he added quickly: "I dunno's you think it was such a good job, either."

"Yes, I do," she murmured, looking straight ahead of her.

"Well," he said, "I tried —"

He did not finish the sentence, and she could think of nothing more to say.

"Ho, there, Dan, step out," he muttered, jerking the bridle. "We ain't home yet. — You cold?" he asked abruptly.

She shook her head, but he drew the cover higher up, and stooped to tuck it in about the ankles. She continued to look straight ahead. Tears of weariness and weakness were dimming her eyes and beginning to run over, but she dared not wipe them away lest he should observe the gesture.

They drove in silence, following the long loops of the descent upon Hamblin, and Mr. Royall did not speak again till they reached the outskirts of the village. Then he let the reins droop on the dashboard and drew out his watch.

"Charity," he said, "you look fair done up, and North Dormer's a goodish way off. I've figured out that we'd do better to stop here long enough for you to get a mouthful of breakfast and then drive down to Creston and take the train."

She roused herself from her apathetic musing. "The train — what train?"

Mr. Royall, without answering, let the horse jog on till they reached the door of the first house in the village. "This is old Mrs. Hobart's place," he said. "She'll give us something hot to drink."

Charity, half unconsciously, found herself getting out of the buggy and following him in at the open door. They entered a decent kitchen with a fire crackling in the stove. An old woman with a kindly face was setting out cups and saucers on the table. She looked up and nodded as they came in, and Mr. Royall advanced to the stove, clapping his numb hands together.

"Well, Mrs. Hobart, you got any breakfast for this young lady? You can see she's cold and hungry."

Mrs. Hobart smiled on Charity and took a tin coffee-pot from the fire. "My, you do look pretty mean," she said compassionately.

Charity reddened, and sat down at the

table. A feeling of complete passiveness had once more come over her, and she was conscious only of the pleasant animal sensations of warmth and rest.

Mrs. Hobart put bread and milk on the table, and then went out of the house: Charity saw her leading the horse away to the barn across the yard. She did not come back, and Mr. Royall and Charity sat alone at the table with the smoking coffee between them. He poured out a cup for her, and put a piece of bread in the saucer, and she began to eat.

As the warmth of the coffee flowed through her veins her thoughts cleared and she began to feel like a living being again; but the return to life was so painful that the food choked in her throat and she sat staring down at the table in silent anguish.

After a while Mr. Royall pushed back his chair. "Now, then," he said, "if you're a mind to go along —" She did not move, and he continued: "We can pick up the noon train for Nettleton if you say so."

The words sent the blood rushing to her face, and she raised her startled eyes to his. He was standing on the other side of the table looking at her kindly and gravely; and suddenly she understood what he was going to say. She continued to sit motionless, a leaden weight upon her lips.

"You and me have spoke some hard

things to each other in our time, Charity; and there's no good that I can see in any more talking now. But I'll never feel any way but one about you; and if you say so we'll drive down in time to catch that train, and go straight to the minister's house; and when you come back home you'll come as Mrs. Royall."

His voice had the grave persuasive accent that had moved his hearers at the Home Week festival; she had a sense of depths of mournful tolerance under that easy tone. Her whole body began to tremble with the dread of her own weakness.

"Oh, I can't —" she burst out desperately.

"Can't what?"

She herself did not know: she was not sure if she was rejecting what he offered, or already struggling against the temptation of taking what she no longer had a right to. She stood up, shaking and bewildered, and began to speak:

"I know I ain't been fair to you always; but I want to be now. . . . I want you to know . . . I want . . ." Her voice failed her and she stopped.

Mr. Royall leaned against the wall. He was paler than usual, but his face was composed and kindly and her agitation did not appear to perturb him.

"What's all this about wanting?" he said as she paused. "Do you know what you really want? I'll tell you. You want to be took home and took care of. And I guess that's all there is to say."

"No . . . it's not all. . . ."

"Ain't it?" He looked at his watch. "Well, I'll tell you another thing. All *I* want is to know if you'll marry me. If there was anything else, I'd tell you so; but there ain't. Come to my age, a man knows the things that matter and the things that don't; that's about the only good turn life does us."

His tone was so strong and resolute that it was like a supporting arm about her. She felt her resistance melting, her strength slipping away from her as he spoke.

"Don't cry, Charity," he exclaimed in a shaken voice. She looked up, startled at his emotion, and their eyes met.

"See here," he said gently, "old Dan's come a long distance, and we've got to let him take it easy the rest of the way. . . ."

He picked up the cloak that had slipped to her chair and laid it about her shoulders. She followed him out of the house, and then walked across the yard to the shed, where the horse was tied. Mr. Royall unblanketed him and led him out into the road. Charity got into the buggy and he drew the cover about her and shook out the reins with a cluck. When they reached the end of the village he turned the horse's head toward Creston.

XVIII

They began to jog down the winding road to the valley at old Dan's languid pace. Charity felt herself sinking into deeper depths of weariness, and as they descended through the bare woods there were moments when she lost the exact sense of things, and seemed to be sitting beside her lover with the leafy arch of summer bending over them. But this illusion was faint and transitory. For the most part she had only a confused sensation of slipping down a smooth irresistible current; and she abandoned herself to the feeling as a refuge from the torment of thought.

Mr. Royall seldom spoke, but his silent presence gave her, for the first time, a sense of peacc and security. She knew that where he was there would be warmth, rest, silence; and for the moment they were all she wanted. She shut her eyes, and even these things grew dim to her. . . .

In the train, during the short run from Creston to Nettleton, the warmth aroused her, and the consciousness of being under strange eyes gave her a momentary energy.

She sat upright, facing Mr. Royall, and stared out of the window at the denuded country. Forty-eight hours earlier, when she had last traversed it, many of the trees still held their leaves; but the high wind of the last two nights had stripped them, and the lines of the landscape were as finely pencilled as in December. A few days of autumn cold had wiped out all trace of the rich fields and languid groves through which she had passed on the Fourth of July; and with the fading of the landscape those fervid hours had faded, too. She could no longer believe that she was the being who had lived them; she was someone to whom something irreparable and over-whelming had happened, but the traces of the steps leading up to it had almost vanished.

When the train reached Nettleton and she walked out into the square at Mr. Royall's side the sense of unreality grew more over-powering. The physical strain of the night and day had left no room in her mind for new sensations and she followed Mr. Royall as passively as a tired child. As in a con-fused dream she presently found herself sitting with him in a pleasant room, at a table with a red and white tablecloth on which hot food and tea were placed. He filled her cup and plate and whenever she lifted her eyes from them she found his resting on her with the same steady tranquil gaze that had reassured and strengthened her when they had faced each other in old Mrs. Hobart's kitchen. As everything else in her consciousness grew more and more confused and immaterial, became more and more like the universal shimmer that dissolves the world to failing eyes, Mr. Royall's presence began to detach itself with rocky firmness from this elusive background. She had always thought of him — when she thought of him at all — as of someone hateful and obstructive, but whom she could outwit and dominate when she chose to make the effort. Only once, on the day of the Old Home Week celebration, while the stray fragments of his address drifted across her troubled mind, had she caught a glimpse of another being, a being so different from the dull-witted enemy with whom she had supposed herself to be living that even through the burning mist of her own dreams he had stood out with startling distinctness. For a moment, then, what he said — and something in his way of saying it — had made her see why he had always struck her as such a lonely man. But the mist of her dreams had hidden him again, and she had forgotten that fugitive impression.

It came back to her now, as they sat at the table, and gave her, through her own immeasurable desolation, a sudden sense of their nearness to each other. But all these feelings were only brief streaks of light in the grey blur of her physical weakness. Through it she was aware that Mr. Royall presently left her sitting by the table in the warm room, and came back after an interval with a carriage from the station — a closed "hack" with sunburnt blue silk blinds — in which they drove together to a house covered with creepers and standing next to a church with a carpet of turf before it. They got out at this house, and the carriage waited while they walked up the path and entered a wainscoted hall and then a room full of books. In this room a clergyman whom Charity had never seen received them pleasantly, and asked them to be seated for a few minutes while witnesses were being summoned.

Charity sat down obediently, and Mr. Royall, his hands behind his back, paced slowly up and down the room. As he turned and faced Charity, she noticed that his lips were twitching a little; but the look in his eyes was grave and calm. Once he paused before her and said timidly: "Your hair's got kinder loose with the wind," and she lifted her hands and tried to smooth back the locks that had escaped from her braid. There was a looking-glass in a carved frame on the wall, but she was ashamed to look at herself in it, and she sat with her hands folded on her knee till the clergyman returned. Then they went out again, along a sort of arcaded passage, and into a low vaulted room with a cross on an altar, and rows of benches. The clergyman, who had left them at the door, presently reappeared before the altar in a surplice, and a lady who was probably his wife, and a man in a blue shirt who had been raking dead leaves on the lawn, came in and sat on one of the benches.

The clergyman opened a book and signed to Charity and Mr. Royall to approach. Mr. Royall advanced a few steps, and Charity followed him as she had followed him to the buggy when they went out of Mrs. Hobart's kitchen; she had the feeling that if she ceased to keep close to him, and do what he told her to do, the world would slip away from beneath her feet.

The clergyman began to read, and on her dazed mind there rose the memory of Mr. Miles, standing the night before in the desolate house of the Mountain, and reading out of the same book words that had the same dread sound of finality:

"I require and charge you both, as ye will answer at the dreadful day of judgment when the secrets of all hearts shall be disclosed, that if either of you know any impediment whereby ye may not be lawfully joined together . . . ."

Charity raised her eyes and met Mr. Royall's. They were still looking at her kindly and steadily. "I will!" she heard him say a moment later, after another interval of words that she had failed to catch. She was so busy trying to understand the gestures that the clergyman was signalling to her to make that she no longer heard what was being said. After another interval the lady on the bench stood up, and taking her hand put it in Mr. Royall's. It lay enclosed in his strong palm and she felt a ring that was too big for her being slipped on her thin finger. She understood then that she was married. . . .

Late that afternoon Charity sat alone in a bedroom of the fashionable hotel where she and Harney had vainly sought a table on the Fourth of July. She had never before been in so handsomely furnished a room. The mirror above the dressing-table reflected the high head-board and fluted pillow-slips of the double bed, and a bed-spread so spotlessly white that she had hesitated to lay her hat and jacket on it. The humming radiator diffused an atmosphere of drowsy warmth, and through a half-open door she saw the glitter of the nickel taps above twin marble basins.

For a while the long turmoil of the night and day had slipped away from her and she sat with closed eyes, surrendering herself to the spell of warmth and silence. But presently this merciful apathy was succeeded by the sudden acuteness of vision with which sick people sometimes wake out of a heavy sleep. As she opened her eyes they rested on the picture that hung above the bed. It was a large engraving with a dazzling white margin enclosed in a wide frame of bird's-eye maple with an inner scroll of gold. The engraving represented a young man in a boat on a lake overhung with trees. He was leaning over to gather water-lilies for the girl in a light dress who lay among the cushions in the stern. The scene was full of a drowsy midsummer radiance, and Charity averted her eyes from it and, rising from her chair, began to wander restlessly about the room.

It was on the fifth floor, and its broad window of plate glass looked over the roofs of the town. Beyond them stretched a wooded landscape in which the last fires of sunset were picking out a steely gleam. Charity gazed at the gleam with startled eyes. Even through the gathering twilight she recognized the contour of the soft hills encircling it, and the way the meadows sloped to its edge. It was Nettleton Lake that she was looking at.

She stood a long time in the window staring out at the fading water. The sight of it had roused her for the first time to a realization of what she had done. Even the feeling of the ring on her hand had not brought her this sharp sense of the irretrievable. For an instant the old impulse of flight swept through her; but it was only the lift of a broken wing. She heard the door open behind her, and Mr. Royall came in.

He had gone to the barber's to be shaved, and his shaggy grey hair had been trimmed and smoothed. He moved strongly and quickly, squaring his shoulders and carrying his head high, as if he did not want to pass unnoticed.

"What are you doing in the dark?" he called out in a cheerful voice. Charity made no answer. He went up to the window to draw the blind, and putting his finger on the wall flooded the room with a blaze of light from the central chandelier. In this unfamiliar illumination husband and wife faced each other awkwardly for a moment; then Mr. Royall said: "We'll step down and have some supper, if you say so."

The thought of food filled her with repugnance; but not daring to confess it she smoothed her hair and followed him to the lift.

An hour later, coming out of the glare of the dining-room, she waited in the marble-panelled hall while Mr. Royall, before the brass lattice of one of the corner counters, selected a cigar and bought an evening paper. Men were lounging in rocking chairs under the blazing chandeliers, travellers coming and going, bells ringing, porters shuffling by with luggage. Over Mr. Royall's shoulder, as he leaned against the counter, a girl with her hair puffed high smirked and nodded at a dapper drummer who was getting his key at the desk across the hall.

Charity stood among these cross-currents of life as motionless and inert as if she had been one of the tables screwed to the marble floor. All her soul was gathered up into one sick sense of coming doom, and she watched Mr. Royall in fascinated terror while he pinched the cigars in successive boxes and unfolded his evening paper with a steady hand.

Presently he turned and joined her. "You go right along up to bed — I'm going to sit down here and have my smoke," he said. He spoke as easily and naturally as if they had been an old couple, long used to each other's ways, and her contracted heart gave a flutter of relief. She followed him to the lift, and he put her in and enjoined the buttoned and braided boy to show her to her room.

She groped her way in through the darkness, forgetting where the electric button was, and not knowing how to manipulate it. But a white autumn moon had risen, and the illuminated sky put a pale light in the room. By it she undressed, and after folding up the ruffled pillow-slips crept timidly under the spotless counterpane. She had never felt such smooth sheets or such light warm blankets; but the softness of the bed did not soothe her. She lay there trembling with a fear that ran through her veins like ice. "What have I done? Oh, what have I done?" she whispered, shuddering to her pillow; and pressing her face against it to shut out the pale landscape beyond the window she lay in the darkness straining her ears, and shaking at every footstep that approached. . . .

Suddenly she sat up and pressed her hands against her frightened heart. A faint sound had told her that someone was in the room; but she must have slept in the interval, for she had heard no one enter. The moon was setting beyond the opposite roofs, and in the darkness outlined against the grey square of the window, she saw a figure seated in the rocking-chair. The figure did not move: it was sunk deep in the chair, with bowed head and folded arms, and she saw that it was Mr. Royall who sat there. He had not undressed, but had taken the blanket from the foot of the bed and laid it across his knees. Trembling and holding her breath she watched him, fearing that he had been roused by her movement; but he did not stir, and she concluded that he wished her to think he was asleep.

As she continued to watch him ineffable relief stole slowly over her, relaxing her strained nerves and exhausted body. He knew, then . . . he knew . . . it was because he knew that he had married her, and that he sat there in the darkness to show her she was safe with him. A stir of something deeper than she had ever felt in thinking of him flitted through her tired brain, and cautiously, noiselessly, she let her head sink on the pillow. . . .

When she woke the room was full of morning light, and her first glance showed her that she was alone in it. She got up and dressed, and as she was fastening her dress the door opened, and Mr. Royall came in. He looked old and tired in the bright daylight, but his face wore the same expression of grave friendliness that had reassured her on the Mountain. It was as if all the dark spirits had gone out of him.

They went downstairs to the dining-room for breakfast, and after breakfast he told her he had some insurance business to attend to. "I guess while I'm doing it you'd better step out and buy yourself whatever you need." He smiled, and added with an embarrassed laugh: "You know I always wanted you to beat all the other girls." He drew something from his pocket, and pushed it across the table to her; and she saw that he had given her two twenty-dollar bills. "If it ain't enough there's more where that come from — I want you to beat 'em all hollow," he repeated.

She flushed and tried to stammer out her thanks, but he had pushed back his chair and was leading the way out of the dining-room. In the hall he paused a minute to say that if it suited her they would take the three o'clock train back to North Dormer; then he took his hat and coat from the rack and went out.

A few minutes later Charity went out, too. She had watched to see in what direction he was going, and she took the opposite way and walked quickly down the main street to the brick building on the corner of Lake Avenue. There she paused to look cautiously up and down the thoroughfare, and then climbed the brass-bound stairs to Dr. Merkle's door. The same bushy-headed mulatto girl admitted her, and after the same interval of waiting in the red plush parlor she was once more summoned to Dr. Merkle's office. The doctor received her without surprise, and led her into the inner plush sanctuary.

"I thought you'd be back, but you've come a mite too soon: I told you to be patient and not fret," she observed, after a pause of penetrating scrutiny.

Charity drew the money from her breast. "I've come to get my blue brooch," she said, flushing.

"Your brooch?" Dr. Merkle appeared not to remember. "My, yes — I get so many things of that kind. Well, my dear, you'll have to wait while I get it out of the safe. I don't leave valuables like that laying round like the noospaper."

She disappeared for a moment, and returned with a bit of twisted-up tissue paper from which she unwrapped the brooch.

Charity, as she looked at it, felt a stir of warmth at her heart. She held out an eager hand.

"Have you got the change?" she asked a little breathlessly, laying one of the twenty-dollar bills on the table.

"Change? What'd I want to have change for? I only see two twenties there," Dr. Merkle answered brightly.

Charity paused, disconcerted. "I thought . . . you said it was five dollars a visit. . . ."

"For *you,* as a favour — I did. But how about the responsibility and the insurance? I don't s'pose you ever thought of that? This pin's worth a hundred dollars easy. If it had got lost or stole, where'd I been when you come to claim it?"

Charity remained silent, puzzled and half-convinced by the argument, and Dr. Merkle promptly followed up her advantage. "I didn't ask you for your brooch, my dear. I'd a good deal ruther folks paid me my regular charge than have 'em put me to all this trouble."

She paused, and Charity, seized with a desperate longing to escape, rose to her feet and held out one of the bills.

"Will you take that?" she asked.

"No, I won't take that, my dear; but I'll take it with its mate, and hand you over a signed receipt if you don't trust me."

"Oh, but I can't — it's all I've got," Charity exclaimed.

Dr. Merkle looked up at her pleasantly from the plush sofa. "It seems you got married yesterday, up to the 'Piscopal church; I heard all about the wedding from the minister's chore-man. It would be a pity, wouldn't it, to let Mr. Royall know you had an account running here? I just put it to you as your own mother might."

Anger flamed up in Charity, and for an instant she thought of abandoning the brooch and letting Dr. Merkle do her worst. But how could she leave her only treasure with that evil woman? She wanted it for her baby: she meant it, in some mysterious way, to be a link between Harney's child and its unknown father. Trembling and hating herself while she did it, she laid Mr. Royall's money on the table, and catching up the brooch fled out of the room and the house. . . .

In the street she stood still, dazed by this last adventure. But the brooch lay in her bosom like a talisman, and she felt a secret lightness of heart. It gave her strength, after a moment, to walk on slowly in the direction of the post office, and go in through the swinging doors. At one of the windows she bought a sheet of letter-paper, an envelope and a stamp; then she sat down at a table and dipped the rusty post office pen in ink. She had come there possessed with a fear which had haunted her ever since she had felt Mr. Royall's ring on her finger: the fear that Harney might, after all, free himself and come back to her. It was a possibility which had never occurred to her during the dreadful hours after she had received his letter; only when the decisive step she had taken made longing turn to apprehension did such a contingency seem conceivable. She addressed the envelope, and on the sheet of paper she wrote:

I'm married to Mr. Royall. I'll always remember you.

CHARITY.

The last words were not in the least what she had meant to write; they had flowed from her pen irresistibly. She had not had the strength to complete her sacrifice; but, after all, what did it matter? Now that there was no chance of ever seeing Harney again, why should she not tell him the truth?

When she had put the letter in the box she went out into the busy sunlit street and began to walk to the hotel. Behind the plate-glass windows of the department stores she noticed the tempting display of dresses and dress-materials that had fired her imagination on the day when she and Harney had looked in at them together. They reminded her of Mr. Royall's injunction to go out and buy all she needed. She looked down at her shabby dress, and wondered what she should say when he saw her coming back empty-handed. As she drew near the hotel she saw him waiting on the doorstep, and her heart began to beat with apprehension.

He nodded and waved his hand at her approach, and they walked through the hall and went upstairs to collect their possessions, so that Mr. Royall might give up the key of the room when they went down again for their midday dinner. In the bedroom, while she was thrusting back into the satchel the few things she had brought away with her, she suddenly felt that his eyes were on her and that he was going to speak. She stood still, her half-folded night-gown in her hand, while the blood rushed up to her drawn cheeks.

"Well, did you rig yourself out hand-somely? I haven't seen any bundles round," he said jocosely.

"Oh, I'd rather let Ally Hawes make the few things I want," she answered.

"That so?" He looked at her thoughtfully for a moment and his eye-brows projected in a scowl. Then his face grew friendly again. "Well, I wanted you to go back look-ing stylisher than any of them; but I guess you're right. You're a good girl, Charity."

Their eyes met, and something rose in his that she had never seen there: a look that made her feel ashamed and yet secure.

"I guess you're good, too," she said, shyly and quickly. He smiled without answering, and they went out of the room together and dropped down to the hall in the glittering lift.

Late that evening, in the cold autumn moonlight, they drove up to the door of the red house.

About the Author

Edith Wharton was born into a distinguished and wealthy New York City family in 1862. Her love of travel and literature was encouraged from a young age, as were the fine manners expected by her family's social circle. Nevertheless, the family did not approve of Wharton's ambitions to become a published author. She married in 1885, but that union was a troubled one. *The House of Mirth* (1905) was her first book to win critical praise. Following the example of her friend Henry James, Wharton decided to live permanently in Europe, settling in France in 1907 and divorcing in 1913. Her career blossomed. Volume after volume of her beautifully crafted fiction appeared over the next thirty years, many dealing with empty, destructive codes of social behavior and the stultifying weight that society places on creative, passionate spirits. Wharton died in France in 1937, one of the most honored writers in American history.